Changing

Seasons

Also by BJ Phillips

Seasons
Hurricane Season
Snowbird Season

Changing Seasons

BJ Phillips

Desert Palm Press

Changing Season
(Seasons – Book 3)

by BJ Phillips

© 2018 by BJ Phillips

ISBN (trade): 9781948327008
ISBN (epub): 9781948327015
ISBN (pdf): 9781948327022

For permission requests, write to the publisher at lee@desertpalmpress.com or "Attention: Permissions Coordinator," at

Desert Palm Press
1961 Main Street, Suite 220
Watsonville, California 95076
www.desertpalmpress.com

Editor: Mary Hettel
Cover Design: eeboxWORX (https://mich-bro.myportfolio.com/projects)

Printed in the United States of America
First Edition July 2018

ACKNOWLEDGEMENTS

Once again, thanks to my publisher, Lee Fitzsimmons at Desert Palm Press, for still believing the stories I write are publishable. Mary Hettel, this book would not be quite what it is without your editing. And Mich Brodeur, thank you for yet another lovely cover. It's a blessing to work with each of you again.

.

DEDICATION

This book, as always, is dedicated to my wonderful partner, Debbie Hilliard. Your encouragement and love make it possible for me to continue to do what I love doing. Thank you so much for continuing to believe in me.

LOVE COMES IN MANY forms. It can't be forced, and it usually comes when we least expect it. The heart can be broken and mended many times and still manage to love the right one when she comes along, if we let it. At least we always hope so.

In our twenties it comes with second glances, longing gazes, and hot sex. In our forties, it can come as a surprise—a beautiful woman trips and falls into our arms, someone we thought we didn't like turns out to be 'the one.' It can still come in our sixties or later, sidling up to us as a friend who becomes a lover.

It's all the same. It's love in all its varieties that still takes our breath away at every age. As well it should.

CHAPTER ONE

ELISE WAINWRIGHT HAD THE coffee on and was waiting for Lauren to arrive. She and Lauren Prescott both looked forward to this morning ritual they started several weeks ago. Lauren lived in the same upscale gated subdivision, only a few streets away.

It was a bit early, so Elise slipped on a pair of yard clogs, picked up her clippers and a pair of gloves from a kitchen drawer, and stepped outside to trim the roses near the front door. She inhaled a deep breath and stretched her arms wide, smiling to herself. Elise loved the morning sounds of the birds calling to one another and the aromas of damp grass, palm trees, and flowers. A light breeze whooshed the fronds on the palm trees in the middle of her expansive circular brick driveway. Within a few minutes, she had deadheaded the two rose bushes and carried in a small bouquet of just-opened rosebuds, which she put in a glass vase on her kitchen's granite counter.

Right on schedule, Elise heard Lauren's Escalade out front. A minute later, Lauren came through the front door without knocking, wearing a huge grin. In her hands was a cardboard container, carried like a crown on a pillow.

"What's that?" Elise pointed to the pink paper box.

"Ah, you're going to love these." Lauren set the box on the island in front of Elise and opened the cover, fanning the aroma toward her.

"Oh, God, warm blueberry muffins! Where did you get them?" Elise reached into the box and removed one of the mini muffins, holding it in her hand like it was a baby bird. She inhaled its aroma, biting into it slowly with her eyes closed. "I could eat a million of these."

Lauren grinned, her grey eyes sparkling. "Believe it or not, I made them."

Elise's eyes snapped open. "No, you didn't. Come on, this is wonderful. I thought you didn't cook." She picked up the box and carried it with her coffee to the small built-in breakfast nook in the corner of her kitchen.

Lauren followed her, then leaned on the island and crossed her arms. "What made you think that? Just because I haven't cooked for you doesn't mean I can't. Besides, Betty Crocker and I work well together. She's one of my best buddies, along with Duncan Hines and Pillsbury."

Elise laughed. "They're nice friends to keep around."

Lauren's grin widened as she slid onto the upholstered bench across from Elise. "You're right, I don't cook much. I am, however, a pretty decent baker of muffins and cookies. You know, stuff out of boxes or refrigerated dough. I'm quite good at cookies. They're great for open houses and make the house or condo I'm showing smell heavenly. It's amazing what a nice cookie smell can do."

Elise reached for a second muffin. "You can do this for me anytime. They're almost sinful, they're so delicious. Oh, my goodness, I'm sorry. I'm sitting here stuffing my face and didn't get you any coffee."

"I know where the coffee pot and the cups are and I'm certainly not helpless. Help yourself to as many of the muffins as you like. I plan to eat several, myself." Lauren reached for a muffin, got back up, and started eating it on the way to the coffee pot. "So, how's Andi doing with organizing the new gallery?" she asked over her shoulder. "It occurred to me yesterday that I haven't seen a grand opening announcement yet."

"She's doing fine. It's going to be a little while yet before you see that announcement. Lining up talent and then setting it all up does take time. The last I heard, she hadn't even gotten an office set up over there and was working off a worktable and folding chairs. When I talked to her earlier this morning, it sounded like she had another idea and was up before dawn again."

Lauren reached for the mug Elise had left on the counter for her and poured herself some coffee. "Wow, that niece of yours is something, isn't she? I don't get into New York often, but I'd love to see her shop there in SoHo. I looked up her website a while back and was very impressed. You've got to be a very proud aunt."

Elise smiled at her between bites of muffin. "Of course, I am. I couldn't be prouder of her if she was my own daughter. She'll have quite a challenge running two places, though, especially since this one will be quite different from the other one. It doesn't help that they're so far apart. When this idea first came to her, she wanted it to specialize in some sort of Florida artwork. Kelly doesn't know yet, but since there's so much here in town already, Andrea's decided to make this one different. It's going to be a showcase of woodworking pieces."

Lauren returned to slide into the bench again as she put down her coffee mug and reached for another muffin. "Now that would be different. Why hasn't she told Kelly? Seems to me the woodworking focus for the new shop would interest her." She popped the muffin into her mouth.

"Yes, it would. Because Kelly's work inspired her to do this, she doesn't want her to think she's pressuring her to make things to sell. Apparently that was one of their misunderstandings in the beginning."

"Hmm... I wasn't aware of that."

"When Andrea saw some handcrafted things Kelly had made for her friends, she said some very nice things about them, coming from her perspective as an art gallery owner. Kelly assumed, from what Andrea said, that she was only interested in her for what she did, not for herself. Andrea had to convince her that wasn't the case." Elise sipped her coffee. "I'm so glad those two got together. They seem very happy."

"Yes, they do. They're both wonderful women and I'm glad to see they found happiness." Lauren reached across the table for Elise's hand. "I'm very glad we found each other."

Elise smiled and put her other hand on top of Lauren's. "So am I. I was sure I had a full life until you came along. You filled a place in my world that I didn't realize was empty. You're a great friend."

Lauren enclosed Elise's hands in both of hers. Her eyes locked onto Elise's bright blue eyes. "You know I think of you as more than a friend. Elise, I truly care for you. We both decided to take our relationship slowly, but do you think we might be ready for more than coffee in the mornings, occasional dates in the evenings, and some outstanding goodnight kisses?"

Elise looked down at their joined hands. "It's been so long. I'm not sure I'm ready for more. Are we too old for this? What if...I mean, maybe...hell, you've got me all tongue-tied." She laughed. "I guess that's a good thing, isn't it?"

"Yes, it is. I'd love to go to sleep simply holding you in my arms. I had in mind that we could spend a night together with no expectation of anything other than keeping each other company. How do you feel about that?"

Elise searched Lauren's grey eyes as if they would give her an answer. "I believe I'd like that too," she whispered.

"See, that wasn't so scary now, was it?" Lauren smiled and tilted her head, waiting for a response.

Elise inhaled a deep breath and let it out slowly. "No, it wasn't. I was afraid we might jump into bed and if it wasn't good, that would be the end of what we share. I don't want to lose having you in my life, especially over sex. I care for you very much and enjoy your company and—"

Lauren interrupted her. "You'll never lose me over sex, believe me. Although I think you're very sexy and I would love to make love to you, that isn't all there is between us. We laugh a lot. We are so much alike in many ways, including that we're very independent and stubborn." That made them both laugh. "I do think we could have more together than we do now. I'd love to go to sleep at night and wake up in the morning with you in my arms. I'm not talking about every night, and I'm not saying we should move in together or something like that. Neither of us is ready for that."

Elise looked at her hands, shook her head slowly, and smiled. "No, we aren't. We both like having our own homes and we're pretty much set in our ways. It's not that it could never happen, although I can't see it happening anytime soon."

"I'm pretty sure I can hear the whir of tiny wheels coming from your head. Want to share your thoughts?" Lauren leaned forward, put her fingers under Elise's chin to lift her face. She gazed into Elise's eyes, waiting for an answer.

"I think maybe we could give it a try. Tell you what, why don't you bring an overnight bag when you come for supper tonight. If it feels right, you can spend the night. It could be like a pajama party."

Lauren grinned. "That sounds great." Her grin disappeared. "Absolutely no pressure, though. If it doesn't feel right tonight or you're too tired, or you realize you're not ready for this, I'll go home as usual and we'll wait until you're ready. How's that?"

"But if it does feel right, then..." Elise's lips lifted in a little smile.

"Then we take it one step at a time." Lauren's grin returned as she reached to stroke the side of Elise's face. She caught a glimpse of her watch. "I'm so sorry. I've got to get moving. We have an early closing this morning and I need to talk to the title company manager first." Lauren reached for a couple more muffins and a napkin. "To eat in the car. You can keep the rest of them. We might want to snack on them this evening...if there are any left by then."

Elise walked Lauren to the door, where Lauren put her arm around her and kissed her, their lips meeting in a soft touch. "I do care for you very much," she whispered into Elise's ear. "See you tonight." Within less than a minute, Lauren was waving as she got into her car. Elise stood watching as Lauren's Escalade made its way down her driveway and then out of sight.

Elise found herself smiling as she closed the front door. She made herself another cup of coffee to take to her office—with one more muffin—and hummed her way down the hall to work.

CHAPTER TWO

"I HAD A THOUGHT," Kelly Bradley said. "It's been a while since we've had anyone over. I was thinking about inviting Shawn and Carrie and Elise and Lauren for a cookout at the house. A couples evening. What do you think?"

Andi Wainwright looked up from unwrapping the take-out hamburger and fries that Kelly had brought to the still almost empty new space. They sat on folding chairs, with an upside-down box as their luncheon table. "That's a great idea. When do you want to do it?"

"I was thinking about having it this Saturday. That way no one has to get up early to go to work."

Andi chewed on her lower lip then offered a wan smile. "Except me."

Kelly's shoulders dropped. "No. What happened?"

"A little while before you got here I got a call from Michael. I need to go back to New York to take care of some things in SoHo. I'm sorry."

"And you need to take an early flight on Sunday? Can't you leave Sunday afternoon like you usually do?"

"I could if there were any seats left. I went online right away, but every seat was gone for the afternoon flights out of Regional Southwest. The only other option would be to charter a plane out of Page Field, however, I'd rather not. I've been lucky so far when I wanted to catch a flight on Sunday later in the day. It looks like my luck finally ran out. I guess a weekend on the beach is over for those tourists with an afternoon flight. It's not a holiday weekend, so I can't imagine why those flights are full. You'd think more people from New York would take the shorter trip to the Jersey shore."

Kelly leaned back in her chair. "I don't blame tourists for wanting to come to our beaches. We have the palm trees, sugary white sand, sunsets over the Gulf, tropical breezes, and all that. I've never been to the Jersey shore, but I can't imagine it can compare with our beaches. Besides, the Jersey shore is on the wrong side."

"Well, it's just different. It's nice, though." She stopped, her brows furrowed. "Wait…the wrong side? The wrong side of what?"

Kelly laughed. "The wrong side of the continent. It faces the wrong way. The sun is supposed to go down over the water, not come up."

Andi shook her head as she laughed. "Interesting perspective. Okay, I get what you're saying. Oddly enough, I've never thought of it that way, even though I've been to both beaches. Looks like I need to take you to the shore one of these days, though. I'm sure you'd enjoy it, even if it is on the wrong side. Aunt Elise knows people with beach houses or condos. I'd bet one of them would be happy to loan me a condo or the like for a holiday whenever we're ready. Of course, there are always beach hotels."

"You mean your aunt doesn't own a beach house up there? I'm shocked!" Kelly put her palms on her face in exaggeration, then laughed. "Actually, I might let you do that sometime. I guess since I grew up here, the idea of going away for a beach vacation has never interested me. Of course, a beautiful woman could persuade me…" She waggled her eyebrows suggestively.

Andi grinned. "Oh, you could be persuaded? Aren't you sweet. I'm sure Aunt Elise never considered a house or condo at the shore in Jersey, since she's had her home here in Florida for what seems like forever. When she's in New York, it's more for work or the holidays nowadays. I don't remember ever hearing her show any interest in a vacation up there during shore season."

"Okay, I get it. Besides, I was mostly giving you a hard time. All right, how about Friday night for the cookout, then? That'd still give our guests several days' notice."

"That sounds good to me. If they insist on bringing something, which they will, we can let Aunt Elise bring a bottle of wine or the like, and Shawn and Carrie can bring some dessert." She thought for a second as she reached for a French fry and dredged it through the ketchup on the open wrapper. A couple of seconds later, she pointed it at Kelly. "Come to think of it, it's been ages since I've had one of Carrie's yummy pies. They're all great, but of course I do love her chocolate pie."

Kelly leaned forward over their makeshift lunch table and took a bite of Andi's fry. "I'll talk to Shawn, then, and you ask Elise. I'll hint about the pie, just for you."

Andi giggled as she stuffed the rest of the fried potato in her mouth. "Aren't you the selfless one…like you don't love Carrie's pies as much as I do."

"Well, yeah, sure I do. I thought it'd sound better if I say you asked for it. Carrie's fond of you."

"I like her a lot too. I remember her calling you her 'knight in shining armor' when I first met her."

"That was sweet of her. I'm sure you're her favorite now, after Piper of course. Carrie adores that little mutt of ours. As far as people go, I think she likes you as much as me—maybe more."

"Piper's such a cutie. Yep, I'm sure she comes first, with everyone else except Shawn coming in a distant second as far as Carrie is concerned. If Piper had fingers instead of a paw, she'd have Carrie wrapped tightly around one of them." Andi sipped from her soda. "All right, you can talk to Shawn. I'll call Aunt Elise right after lunch while it's fresh on my mind. Guess we'd better finish eating so we can both get back to work." She held up the rest of her sandwich. "By the way, did I thank you for bringing me sustenance?"

Kelly's head tilted as she thought for a second. "Now that you mention it, I don't think you did."

She nodded as a slight bow. "Thank you. It was nice of you."

"No big thing. I knew you'd appreciate something to eat. I was hungry and since I was doing the drive-thru thing anyway, I decided I'd rather eat lunch with you than by myself. I had two options—enjoy a meal with you here in this nice air-conditioned space, or on my tailgate at the renovation worksite. You won, hands down."

"So, you're after me for my air conditioning now, huh? I guess that's okay. Would you take a kiss for payment?"

Kelly grinned. "Oh, yeah. Any time!"

Andi grinned back and leaned forward as she paid Kelly her due. Their lips met in a soft, sweet kiss. "Mmm...that was nice. I guess it's a good thing you did bring me some lunch, or I probably would've forgotten to eat again. What would I do without you? I—" she cut herself off.

"You what?"

"I...uh...I do care about you very much."

"I care about you too."

"I know."

BJ Phillips

CHAPTER THREE

SHAWN RICHARDS SAT BACK in her desk chair, stretching her arms up and out. Her forty-year-old back told her it was time to take a break. Close to finishing her latest romance novel, she'd made good progress this afternoon. As often as she'd been to Sanibel Island over the years, it looked like she was going to need another trip out there to check a few details. Her local readers were sure to catch any mistake, and she wasn't going to let that happen again. Besides, who wouldn't mind a morning or an afternoon on Sanibel, where a walk on the beach was always wonderful?

On her way to the kitchen, she heard a vehicle out front. She did a one-eighty and got to the window in time to see Kelly's Durango stop in the driveway. She met her best friend as Kelly opened the door to the screened-in front porch of her cracker house.

Kelly grinned when she saw her. "I hope I didn't interrupt your work. I wouldn't want to bother you in the middle of some steamy love scene."

Shawn grabbed Kelly in a hug, and then released her. "Hey, you! No, you didn't. I'd just decided to take a break from my imaginary world when I heard you drive up. Would you like a soda or some sweet tea? I was going for some tea, myself," she said as they stepped into the house and closed the door.

"You know me. I can always go for some sweet tea."

A few minutes later, iced tea glasses in hand, they settled into chairs on the front porch. They sat for a bit in silence, enjoying the breeze coming through the old painted metal screens and the rustling of the palm tree fronds.

Kelly sighed as she leaned back in her chair and put her feet up on the ledge at the bottom of the screen. "Do you realize this spot right here is where we've solved a lot of problems?" She took in a deep breath and let it out in another long sigh. "It's nice to sit here without having a problem to solve."

"Yes, it is. So, is something up or did you come over solely to sit on my porch? It's okay if you did, and I wouldn't blame you at all if that's why you're here." Shawn sipped from her glass.

"I have to admit I love sitting here. It's nice and quiet most of the time. The real reason I'm here, though, is that we miss you and Carrie. It seems like it's been ages since we've seen you two, so we'd like you to come over for a cook-out on Friday. Are you guys up for that?"

"We miss you too. Carrie and I were talking about that at dinner last night. I guess we've all been rather busy lately. I'll check with her, but I'm pretty sure we can. What would you like us to bring?"

Kelly grinned. "Well..." She drew the word out.

"Well, what? I can kind of guess what you want. Spit it out." Shawn started grinning.

"Would it be too much to ask for Carrie to make one of those famous pies of hers? Andi said she'd love it if Carrie has time to make one. If not, you could bring something else for dessert."

"Yeah, I figured you'd say that." Shawn chuckled some more. "Did Andi request a specific pie? Chocolate, for instance?"

"Yes, as a matter of fact Andi did happen to mention that it'd be especially nice if Carrie had time to make her favorite. She's been in love with that chocolate pie since the first time she tasted it."

Shawn nodded. "I get that. Since I happen to like that one too, I'll ask her. If she has time, I'm sure she'd love to make one for you guys. Of course, I'd get to eat some."

Kelly chuckled. "Well, yeah. Everyone knows that's your absolute favorite. If I remember correctly, Carrie hooked you with that pie."

"I'm not sure I'd say 'hooked,' but it was definitely a plus. I admit I love it."

"Great. I'll tell Andi. By the way, we're also inviting Andi's aunt Elise and my real estate agent, Lauren. Have you met Lauren?"

"I don't believe I have. I've seen her picture in the real estate section of the newspaper, of course. I've heard you talk about her a lot, so I sort of feel like I know her. I'm pretty sure that's as close as I've come to meeting her."

"I couldn't remember. She's been dating Elise for a while now. We thought it'd be nice to have our closest friends and family all together at once."

"Geez, it looks like it has been a while since we've talked. Andi's aunt is such a pleasant woman when you meet her, and Carrie's always said very nice things about her. I'm glad she has someone special in her life now. Is it serious?"

"It appears that way." Kelly shrugged. "I'm not sure what the two of them think. Lauren's face lights up when she talks about Elise, and Elise simply glows when Lauren's either around or discussed. They've been going out or spending a lot of time together for a while now. Personally, I'd say it's already more than 'like,' but I doubt either of them is ready to say it yet. Lauren's last relationship was quite a bust and from what Andi's said, Elise has been burned badly, as well. I'm sure they're taking their time and I certainly wouldn't blame them if they were."

Shawn sipped of her tea, then set the glass on the floor next to her chair. "Speaking of 'saying it,' how are you two doing? It's obvious you're smitten with Andi and she with you. I mean, you two even moved in together. Have you finally broken down and told her you love her?"

Kelly ran her fingers through her short blonde hair. "I've come close but I...well, I haven't yet. I guess I want to tell her when it's perfect."

Shawn threw up her hands. "Geez, woman. What's the hold up? Just tell her. Carrie and I wound up telling each other out in the yard after Hurricane Grace, of all things. I did propose to her in the moonlight on a Sanibel beach, although the 'I love you' came when it came. You shouldn't wait. Really."

"I know. I know. I'm sure Andi loves me, and she's almost told me a couple of times. I'm sure she's waiting for me to say it first, after all we've been through."

"You two are something else. I thought I was bad, the way I acted with Carrie in the beginning. Are you both still dancing around some trust issues after all this time?"

"No, we're not." Kelly was quiet for a few seconds, staring down into her tea glass. She looked back up at Shawn. "No, we definitely aren't. I have no idea why I even had to consider that answer. We're doing great, as a matter of fact. Everything seems almost perfect."

"Then..." Shawn prompted.

"She's still working on setting up that new gallery downtown. She's getting up at all hours with ideas and sometimes staying up late." Kelly set her tea on the floor and stood up, leaning against the porch post. "We don't seem to have much time together right now. I feel like Andi's driving herself into the ground and I worry about her."

Shawn leaned forward in her chair, picking up her ice tea glass and holding it in both hands, her elbows on her knees. "Have you talked to her about it? I mean, if you're truly concerned..."

"I'm trying to let her work it out. The idea is that she's working hard to get this thing going so there'll be more time for us. In the meantime, there's hardly an hour that goes by that she isn't going on and on about this new project."

"Ah. I see." Shawn nodded.

Kelly threw her hands up. "What? What do you see?" she asked. "Do you think I'm feeling left out or ignored?" She began to pace.

"Are you?" Shawn raised her eyebrows, watching her friend.

Kelly stopped pacing, let out a long sigh, and resumed leaning against the post with her hands in her cargo shorts pockets. "Yes, in a way. I also think she's—what's the term—burning her candle at both ends. I'm seriously afraid Andi's going to collapse. A human being has only so much energy, and ninety percent of it is being used on that new gallery. She wouldn't even stop for lunch if I didn't bring her something."

Shawn sipped at her tea. "Maybe it's not as bad as it sounds. I've been known to work through lunch before, and it didn't kill me."

"Well, you don't carry at most 115 pounds on a five-foot-five frame, either, do you?" Kelly winced when she realized how that came out. "Sorry, I didn't mean it the way it sounded."

"You're right, I don't weigh 115 pounds. Missing lunch occasionally wouldn't hurt me at all. Does she eat breakfast?"

She shook her head. "Not really. A bagel, maybe, and some coffee. It sometimes seems like if I wasn't on her case, she'd wouldn't eat because she'd forget."

"What about supper?"

"She does eat supper, although sometimes she only picks at it. When I say something to her about it, she shrugs it off and says, "I'm fine." I can tell that she's lost weight since we've been together. I'm beginning to worry that she might've taken on more than she can handle, or that she needs to get some help setting up the new place. I've offered to help, but of course I can only do the grunt work. I've no idea what else to do."

Shawn nodded. "I can see why you'd be worried. Can you talk to her aunt? From what you and Carrie have said, they're very close. Maybe Elise could do something."

"I'd actually hate to do that. It'd feel like I was going behind Andi's back, kind of like she was a kid and I was telling on her. If I don't see any improvement by Friday night, though, I might take Elise aside and mention my concerns to her then. Of course, it's possible Elise might notice Andi's weight loss on her own and say something to her."

"That's a good idea."

"Every so often I do have a good one." Kelly smiled a little.

Shawn patted Kelly's chair. "How about for now you sit down now and relax for a few minutes?"

"You're right." Kelly lowered herself into the porch chair and leaned her head back against the wall for a moment. "All right, I'm more relaxed." She grinned at Shawn while reaching for her iced tea. Shawn watched and waited as Kelly gulped down a few swallows. "I'm not used to this heavy-duty relationship thing. I like it and I'm getting used to it, though. God knows Andi is the one I want it with. Is it always this tiring?"

Shawn laughed. "Hell, no! If it was, I don't think anyone would bother." Her look became serious. "You're going through a rough time right now. It'll get better, I'm sure."

"You are, huh? Andi wants to get this new thing going, but..." Kelly breathed in deeply and let it out in a sigh, leaning her head back against the house once more. "This is such a hard patch."

"Sounds like it." Shawn thought for a minute as she stared out across her front yard. The only sounds were the rustling of palm fronds and the scratchy sound of squirrels running up and down the tree trunks. "Look, from where I sit, you're amazingly good for each other. For what it's worth, my advice is to hang on. I'm sure it'll get easier. Once that new gallery is opened and running, she can hire employees to handle some of the daily stuff if she wants to."

"True. I can see that Andi's trying. I worry about her constantly, though, and this whole situation feels like it's wearing me out. Plus, we barely have any time together, if you know what I mean." Kelly swallowed a couple of long swigs from her tea as Shawn waited. "Anyway, she thought this cookout was a great idea, so I hope that means she'll make more time to relax."

"Look, I realize that I get involved with my work and sometimes I'm not even aware of what planet I'm on. If I look like I'm getting overly tired or Carrie thinks I need a little break, she'll bring me a glass of tea or a cup of coffee and remind me to walk away, even if it's just for a little while. There are occasions when I need to keep going because I'm in a good place. Carrie has learned the difference. I guess you'll need to learn that with Andi. The trick is don't let it go on too long. Like you said, she doesn't have a lot of reserve to fall back on like you and I do." Shawn patted her not quite flat stomach and laughed.

Kelly let out a sigh. "No, she doesn't. It appears there's less reserve all the time, and I'm afraid she might burn out."

CHAPTER FOUR

"I'M SORRY I DIDN'T cook for you tonight." Elise put down her fork. "I planned to, but I got busy and..."

Lauren laughed. "Good grief, do you think I care that this wasn't home cooked? How many times have I cooked for you? None, except for baking those little muffins. Besides, you hardly need to apologize for takeout from one of my favorite restaurants. I had no idea Nappe Bleu even did takeout, let alone delivery."

"They don't, usually." Elise grinned. "I happen to be friendly with the chef and made special arrangements. The delivery man was leaving when you got here. Did you like the escargot?"

"You're full of surprises. You never told me you knew their chef." Lauren winced. "And to tell you the truth, I'm not big on snails. They're one of the things on the menu I'd never even considered trying. Since you had them here, I did. The creamy garlic sauce made them a bit more palatable than I imagined they'd be. Let's just say I don't think I want them again."

Elise stroked Lauren's arm and nodded. "No problem. Tell you what, I won't expect you to eat them again. Since I like them, I thought they'd be a nice appetizer. You're not required to like everything I do."

"I know. I thought that since we do have very similar tastes, I'd at least give them a try. I had to eat sushi once because a friend treated me to this wonderful little bistro. She said I didn't like it because I'd never had great sushi. She was wrong. I didn't like it because I don't care for sushi. I ate it to please her, but I'd never do it again."

"At least you gave it a try. You're being a good sport about it. I was positive you'd like those chicken crepes, though. You had them the first time we had dinner there and you said they were your favorite thing on their menu. I figured I couldn't go wrong with them."

"Wow. You're good. You remembered what I ate?" Lauren leaned forward. "That was the first place we went out to dinner that wasn't a fundraiser of some kind. I guess our first date, sort of, was that dinner thing I had to go to the day we met. It wasn't much of a date, I admit. I did take you out for dessert and coffee afterward though."

Elise smiled. "Yes, you did. I enjoyed that whole evening with you."

Lauren returned the smile. "I'm glad."

"I'm very comfortable around you. It doesn't matter if we're out somewhere or simply sitting on the lanai having coffee or a glass of wine, talking about whatever. I don't feel the need to make small talk to fill silences in conversation. I don't think about what I'm wearing. You aren't like that."

"You could wear nothing at all and I'd be happy." Lauren clapped her hand over her mouth. "I shouldn't have said that. My mouth opened and...I'm sorry."

Elise gazed into Lauren's grey eyes. "It's all right. No one has said anything like that to me in a very, very long time."

"I didn't mean it. No, I did mean it, although I didn't mean for it to come out the way it sounded. Good grief, now you've got me sputtering."

"Stop apologizing. It's okay." Elise grinned. "How about another glass of the Chardonnay they brought to drink with this? I've never been a big fan of Chardonnay, however, this one's quite good."

Lauren looked at her through squinted eyes. "Are you trying to get me tipsy?"

Elise shook her head, laughing. "Tipsy? I haven't heard anyone use that word since my grandfather said it. And no, I'm not trying to get you inebriated or anything like that."

"Damn." Lauren snapped her fingers. "I thought maybe you were going to get me sauced and then try to take advantage of my situation."

"You wish, but not tonight." Elise laughed. "Tonight, it's feeling quite right for some snuggle time in pj's. How's that?"

"Very nice." Lauren grinned. "I'm happy with that. In fact, I'm more than happy with that." She reached across the table and took Elise's hand, stroking the back of it with her thumb. "I'm glad you decided to be a little more adventurous. You told me it's been a long time since...well, since you've been with anyone. Right now, I'm so looking forward to some pillow talk and just holding you in my arms as we go to sleep."

"I'm looking forward to that too. First things first, let's have dessert. I'm sure you're going to love this." Elise made a show of getting up and going to the kitchen with their dinner plates. Upon her return, she bore a small tray with two little blue bowls containing something fluffy and brown and two dessert spoons.

"No, you didn't…" Lauren leaned over to look as Elise put the tray down.

"Yes, I did. I figured we might as well do it right. I love chocolate mousse, and of course theirs is to die for." She set one of the bowls and a dessert spoon in front of Lauren, and then one of each for herself.

"Oh my God, yes, it is. Merely looking at it makes my mouth water. Thank you." Lauren leaned over to give Elise a little kiss and with a happy sigh, reached for her spoon.

"I thought that mousse might make you happy. It seemed like the perfect way to end supper, especially since I shamelessly ate the rest of those muffins you made."

"Oh, that's all right. I didn't need to eat any more of them. I should pay closer attention to my not-so-girlish figure."

They lifted the bowls and clinked them together as a toast. A few seconds later, they were both making happy noises as they slowly enjoyed spoonful after spoonful of the delectable treat. They topped it off with another kiss, their lips still tasting of chocolate.

Lauren licked her lips. "Mmm…if your kisses always tasted like that chocolate mousse I'd be even more addicted to them than I already am, if that's possible."

"Aren't you the sweet-talker. Speaking of sweet, that mousse was exceptional. I'm going to make sure I order some the next time we go there." Elise stood up. "All right let's put this stuff back in the box it came in, and put it out front for them to come pick up. Then we can move on to other things."

"Shouldn't we wash those dishes?"

"They said not to. They'll throw them in with the rest of the restaurant stuff. On second thought, maybe we should rinse them at least."

"Sounds like a great idea. I'll help."

A short while later, the supper items repacked into the delivery box they came in and a thank you note written to the chef, they put the box on the front step. Elise texted the chef for pickup and thanked him again.

As Elise closed the door behind her, Lauren pulled her close. "Thank you for a wonderful supper." She kissed Elise on the forehead. "It was so thoughtful of you to go to all that trouble." She kissed her on her left cheek. "And I won't forget it." She kissed her on her right cheek. "That only tells me again what a wonderful woman you are and how lucky I am that you're in my life." After kissing Elise's lips softly, she backed away a step.

Elise smiled. "Wow, all that for a take-out supper? I'll have to remember that. For now, though, how about a movie on TV? One of my favorites is on the classic movies channel tonight—How to Marry a Millionaire."

"I love that movie! It cracks me up every time. Even though I know it's coming, that thing at the end where they all think they married poor and it turns out Lauren Bacall's character married an extremely rich guy after all and the girls faint...now that's funny. I laugh every time."

"Me too. Okay, how about we change into pajamas and watch TV in my bedroom? We can be comfortable and cuddle during the movie. How's that?"

Lauren grinned. "We could bring one more glass of wine with us. I'd hate to waste the rest of that bottle."

"Let's do that. There's probably at least one more glass apiece in it. Wait a second." Elise went back to the living room and turned off the lights before picking up the wine bottle and their two glasses. Joining Lauren in the entryway, she motioned for her to follow her down the hall. Lauren picked up her overnight bag and did as she was asked.

CHAPTER FIVE

ELISE STOPPED IN FRONT of a set of double doors, turned to face Lauren, and looked up into her eyes. "I haven't brought anyone to my room except Andrea for a very long time. It's always been my sanctuary."

"Then I'm even more honored to be the one you're inviting in." Lauren placed a little kiss on Elise's lips.

Elise opened the door into a large bedroom, decorated in white wood and wicker. The space was warmed with splashes of pale green, coral, and pale blue in the bedspread, love seat pillows, and in the throw rugs set on the white tile floors. It was elegant, yet comfortable at the same time. A set of French doors led out into what appeared to be a small walled garden. From the bedroom door could be seen a white wicker chair and lounger, their cushions covered in the same fabric as the bedspread. Between them was a white wicker side table, perfect for a book and a coffee cup or wine glass.

"Elise, this room is beautiful. You decorated this yourself, didn't you? It looks like you—warm, comfortable, and elegant at the same time."

Elise smiled. "Thank you. I did all the decorating in the house. I didn't want someone else's idea of what should be in here. This is my favorite room, though, and I wanted it to be my retreat and all about me." She walked over to the little sofa table in front of the love seat and set the wine and glasses down. She gestured to Lauren to follow with her bag, leading the way to a door that wasn't visible from the hall. As she opened the door, lights automatically came on.

Elise waved her hand around the room. "You might like this room, too. You can change in here." Her bathroom was much larger than average with the focal point being a large jetted tub. A separate oversized shower and a long vanity with part of it set up with a chair and extra mirrors completed the room, along with a door leading to the toilet. This room shared the same color scheme as the bedroom.

"Not bad. Not bad at all," Lauren said. "I have a tub like that in mine. Don't you just love those jets?"

"I do. So, yours is big enough for two, also?" Elise leaned against the sink counter and folded her arms. "I've no idea what possessed me to buy such a big tub, but I sure do love it. I take a bubble bath in that thing at least once a week."

Lauren put down her overnight bag. "I haven't tried bubbles in mine. I'll admit that I've never even thought of it. After a long day of open houses, though, I sure do look forward to those warm jets on my body, along with a nice long soak, a good book, and a glass of merlot. Having a hot tub in the back yard isn't quite the same, is it?"

"Nope, not at all. I must say it's a whole different feel with no bathing suit on. I don't have a tub like this one in my New York home, and I definitely miss it when I'm there."

"Then stay here. All the time." Lauren reached for Elise. "It's clear you love being here. You have a beautiful office right down the hall and can telecommute to your editing job at the publishing house, you know. Besides, someday you won't want to work anymore, right?"

"We can talk about that some other time." Elise smiled again, stepping back as she held Lauren's hands. "Right now, why don't you change into your pj's, I'll go change into mine, and we'll meet in the middle at the loveseat. I won't be long." Elise pulled the bathroom door closed behind her and headed for her closet.

Elise's walk-in closet was the size of a bedroom in many homes, holding her built-in dressers and shelves for folded items, as well as her hanging space for clothes, racks for shoes, and shelves for handbags and the like. A large hassock upholstered in the same tropical fabric as her bedspread and a free-standing full-length mirror completed the dressing room.

As Elise began disrobing, she caught a glimpse of herself in the mirror and quickly looked away. For a 60-something, she was in good shape. It just seemed that at that moment every flaw was magnified, including some things that were a lot firmer a decade ago. It hadn't mattered as much before; however, now that she was close to letting someone see her as she was, she wasn't sure it was such a good idea. What if Lauren thought she wasn't sexy enough? That little paunch that never seemed to bother her before now looked like she was in her second trimester. That tiny bit of skin under her arms that wasn't as tight before suddenly looked like turkey wattle. Her breasts weren't quite as firm as they used to be, and neither was her behind. She couldn't offer Lauren the body that she'd once had.

She couldn't deny it, there was more than friendship and a little kissing between them. She knew she wanted more than some cuddling. But it had been so long. It had been decades since she'd been with anyone. What if she just couldn't...well, she wasn't going to think any more about that right now. Tonight was for cuddling only. She slid one leg then the other into her baby blue pajama legs, reveling in the feel of the silk against her skin. She buttoned the short sleeved top and glanced once more at herself, running her fingers through her short greying hair.

Elise opened the door from her dressing room. Lauren was sitting on the love seat wearing similar tailored pajamas in a light green, which complimented her strawberry blonde hair. Elise watched her for a minute as she poured two glasses of wine. The thought came to her that Lauren looked perfectly at home there in her bedroom.

Lauren looked up and noticed her. She raised her eyebrows and grinned. "Wow, it looks like we have similar taste in pajamas, too, although they look much better on you. You look lovely." Lauren handed one of the glasses to Elise. "One thing surprises me, though. I sort of figured you for the negligee type."

Elise laughed and shook her head. "Me? In a negligee? Oh, no, I don't think so. Way too frilly and besides, those things get wrapped around you during the night and get tangled up. Maybe I shouldn't tell you this..." She lowered her voice to a near whisper. "I normally don't wear anything when I'm sleeping."

"Hmm...you sleep in the nude. So do I, usually. Obviously, we won't do that tonight."

"No, we won't. While Andrea lived with me, I always slept in pajamas because I never knew when she was going to need me or want to crawl into bed with me during the night. After she left, I went back to my old ways. It's nice to lie around sometimes in comfy pajamas, though, isn't it?"

Lauren nodded, grinned, and then chuckled.

"And just what's so funny, may I ask?" Elise sipped her wine.

"Have you noticed that we're suddenly making small talk about everything except the fact that we are about to climb into your bed?"

Elise felt her cheeks warm, aware they'd immediately turned bright red.

"Elise, I've never been one for jumping in and out of bed with lots of women. We're simply going to watch TV and cuddle in your bed, then go to sleep in each other's arms and wake up together. That's it. If you're already uncomfortable with this, then maybe I'd better leave now. Or if you'd rather, we can go watch TV in the living room. I honestly don't want you to feel weird about this, and I won't think any less of you if you change your mind."

Elise reached for Lauren's hand. "No, I'm good. I'm glad you're here and I want you to stay. I guess I'm just nervous."

Lauren kissed the hand holding hers. "I never want you to do anything you're not ready for. I make no apologies for saying I want you, because I do. I want you in my life, but I want you on your terms. Please remember that. Going forward by inches is better than not going forward at all, don't you think?"

"Yes, I do. And thank you. Now let's get that movie on. I sleep on the side toward the bathroom, so you get the other side."

They both climbed into bed and settled their wineglasses onto the bedside tables. They piled and propped up the pillows so they could watch the movie. Once Elise got the television set to the right channel, Lauren held out her arm for her. Elise settled into her shoulder with Lauren's arm around her like they'd been doing this their whole lives.

Snuggled into Lauren's arms, she felt something she hadn't felt in a long time—secure. "I've never told you why I haven't had anyone special in my life for a long time." Elise spoke softly, almost whispering. "I'd like to tell you now."

"You do realize you don't have to explain anything to me, right?" Lauren's hand gently stroked Elise's back and shoulder.

"Yes, but I want to tell you. Years ago, I was in a wonderful relationship. Her name was Beth. We'd been together for about ten years, and I truly thought it would last forever. I was in love with her and she had me convinced she loved me just as much. I also had a close friend, Judy, that I'd known since college. Judy and I had been best friends for years. Where I was more reserved, Judy was brash and outgoing—sort of a wild child. Off and on, Beth and I used to hang out with Judy and whoever was her latest fling. Then Beth decided she should fix Judy up with someone stable and she made it her objective to find that perfect woman for her. Unfortunately, one day I came home to find them together in our bed. It seems they had decided they were perfect for each other and were having an affair while Beth was still with me."

Lauren grimaced. "Wow. I know that genuinely sucked. I'm sorry."

"Yeah, thanks." Elise sighed deeply. "It did, and big time. Not only did I lose my partner, I also lost my best friend—the person you usually go to for comfort when something lousy like that happens. I couldn't believe they did that. That was beyond betrayal."

Lauren continued to stroke Elise's shoulder gently as she mulled it over. "Well, I can understand how that might put you off relationships for a while, maybe even for a few years. I seem to remember you commenting once that you've been alone for quite some time. If you don't mind my asking, how long have you been single?"

"More like decades. I went out on a few dates, but I didn't want to get involved in another relationship. I couldn't trust anyone enough. By then, Andrea was living with me and I didn't have the time to devote to anyone else, with work and all. Most of the women I went out with by that time weren't interested in someone raising a child. Anyway, since I was busy working my way up the food chain at the publishing house, I hardly had time for a relationship."

"I'm sorry."

"Don't be. I've had a full life." Elise sat up enough to look at Lauren. "Or at least I thought I did, until I met you." She gave Lauren a little kiss. "You are definitely special."

"Mmm...so are you. You didn't have to tell me all that, but I'm glad you did. It explains what made you so skittish about getting involved with me. I want you to know in your heart I'd never do something like that to you. Ever. That's not my style and never will be. I care for you a lot."

"I know. I care very much for you too."

As the movie began, Elise relaxed into Lauren's embrace with her head on Lauren's chest. From time to time she could hear that low, throaty laugh that had first caught her attention and made her smile. As the movie went on, Elise could hear her breathing, the regular in and out lulling her into a sweet slumber before the movie ended.

Elise woke up the next morning still cuddled next to Lauren, a smile lingering on her lips. It had been so long since she had awakened with anyone in her bed, and even longer since she woke up cuddling with someone. A single tear crept down her cheek as she remembered why, and quickly brushed it away. That was the past. Lauren could very well be her future if she let her.

CHAPTER SIX

KELLY PUT DOWN THE drywall knife, wiped her face on her T-shirt, and picked up her water jug. Time for a little break and hopefully a nice breeze on the front steps of the house she was renovating. It was getting harder to find older houses like this that had good bones and hadn't been neglected to the point of no return. This one was a real treasure in disguise and she enjoyed giving it a new life.

She picked up her insulated jug and was in the middle of taking several swallows of ice water when her phone went off with the distinctive tone that told her Andi was on the other end. She grabbed for it, knowing Andi didn't usually call her in the middle of the day just to chat.

"Hi, sweetie. What's up?"

Andi's voice was breathy. "Actually, I'm not feeling so hot. I'm not sure what's wrong, but I don't think I can drive home. Can you come get me?"

Kelly jumped up and grabbed her keys out of her pocket. "I'll be right there. Is the front door unlocked?" As she talked, she made short work of putting everything on the porch inside, locked the door to the house, and trotted across the porch and down the stairs to her Durango.

"It is now. I'll sit here and wait for you. You're at the project, right?"

"I was. I locked the door and as we speak I'm getting into the truck. I'll be there in a few minutes. What's happening? Keep talking to me."

"I'm not sure. I feel dizzy and nauseated."

"I'm sorry, that sure doesn't sound like fun." Kelly started the engine and backed it out of the driveway.

"Believe me, it's not." Andi's voice sounded a little fainter.

Kelly swallowed hard. "Andi, honey, keep talking to me."

"Okay."

"Where are you? Tell me you're sitting down."

"Yeah, I'm sitting down. Folding chair."

"Can you see the front door from where you are sitting?"

"Yes." Andi was silent for a few seconds. "I've got to go throw up again."

"Okay, I'm almost there. Don't hang up. Just go."

Kelly heard the phone being set down on what was probably one of the metal folding chairs, then hurried footsteps and a door slamming. Within another two minutes, Kelly pulled open the shop door, her eyes scanning the room for her love. Then the sounds of retching reached her from behind the bathroom door.

"Andi, are you in there?" Kelly yelled through the door, and then felt silly. *Of course she was in there. Who else was throwing up in that bathroom?* "Can I help you?" *Yeah, that was another stupid question. Andi can throw up all by herself.* "I mean, is there anything I can do?"

A faint voice from behind the door said, "I'm okay. I think I'm done puking now." Kelly heard the sound of water running. A minute or so later, the handle turned, and the bathroom door opened. Andi's flushed cheeks looked even redder in her nearly colorless face.

"You look awful." Kelly instantly regretted saying that. "I mean, you look like you feel awful." She put her arm around Andi's waist, helped her to a chair, and sat down facing her as she reached for her hand. As soon as Kelly touched Andi's hand, she noticed immediately that it felt cool and clammy. "What happened? You seemed fine this morning."

"I was fine this morning. I've no idea what happened. I feel awful." Andi looked like she was going to fall out of the chair.

Kelly stood up. "Okay, I'm taking you to urgent care. Where are your keys? I'll lock up here."

"They're in my pocket, here." Andi patted her right front jeans pocket and tried to get her keys out, but couldn't. "My bag is over there." She pointed to a box in the corner of the room.

Kelly reached into Andi's pocket, retrieved the keys, and put them in her own pocket. She picked up Andi's bag and returned to get Andi. "Can you stand up?" Kelly put her arm around Andi's waist.

"I'm so sorry, honey." Andi's voice wasn't much more than a whisper. "I'm sure you're busy today."

Kelly lifted Andi to standing position, reached under her knees, and picked her up in her arms. "Don't be silly. You're far more important than anything else I was going to do."

Andi put her arms around Kelly's neck and snuggled her face into her shoulder. "I feel...so awful. And here you are...knight in shining armor...like I knew you'd be. Carrie was so right about you."

"I'm not sure about this knight thing. Let's just get you into the truck. You definitely need more than going home."

"Kelly, I need to tell you something. Now."

"No, not now. Hang on a minute." She put Andi down, helped her slide into the passenger seat, and tilted the seat back slightly. She settled Andi's bag on the floor in front of her and belted her in. "I'll be right back," she told her, shutting the truck door.

Kelly returned to the gallery and quickly locked the door. She looked in the cargo area of her truck for a plastic bag, which she found and handed to Andi. "Just in case. Now close your eyes, or the movement of the truck might make you sick again. If you need me to stop, all you have to do is tell me, okay?" As Andi nodded, Kelly pulled out of the parking space and into the street, making easy, slow turns.

Andi put the bag in her lap and leaned her head back on the headrest and closed her eyes. "I can't...believe...this is happening." Her words were slow, slurred. "Was...fine...this...morning."

Kelly felt her stomach tighten as she listened to her. "Has this ever happened to you before?"

"No. Oh, I'm not sure now. Kelly, I need...tell you..." She turned her head toward Kelly and tried to open her eyes, then closed them again.

Kelly's stomach rolled over. Andi sounded worse by the minute. "Honey, please relax. You don't need to talk right now. We're skipping the urgent care and I'm taking you straight to the emergency room."

Andi appeared to take a deep breath. "I love you." She said it clearly.

Kelly swallowed. This wasn't how she wanted to tell Andi how she felt about her. She wanted a moonlit beach and everything that came with it. She wanted it to be perfect. This wasn't perfect—not by a long shot. It was obvious it was not going to wait. Andi needed to hear it now.

She reached over and grasped Andi's hand, which still felt cold and sweaty at the same time. "I love you too."

Andi's lips curled into a slight smile. "I knew it. Knew...you...loved me. I...wanted...tell you. Wanted...to hear you...say it."

"I'm so sorry. I should've told you a long time ago." Kelly kissed the back of Andi's hand, then put it back in her lap. Kelly brushed away a tiny tear and put both of her own hands on the wheel as she sped up a little. She tried to keep her mind on driving, but it raced along by itself into the dark territory of what-ifs. *What if something happens to her? What if I hadn't heard the phone with my power equipment on? What if...*

A couple of minutes later, they reached the Lee Memorial Hospital Emergency Room entrance. Kelly raced around to the passenger side of the car, unbuckled Andi, and snatched Andi's bag from the floor. Without even trying to rouse her, she picked her up from the car seat and carried her into the emergency room. Her stomach clenched as she felt Andi's clammy body through her clothes. It felt like Andi had passed out.

Someone saw Kelly carrying Andi in, and they came running with a gurney. Kelly quickly laid Andi on it. A nurse asked her what was wrong, and Kelly explained that Andi had a sudden feeling of nausea and dizziness and was now cold and clammy and had slurred speech. They whisked Andi away while Kelly nearly trotted along behind to keep up. Once they were in a treatment room, Kelly pulled the phone from her pocket and punched in Elise's number while the nurse checked Andi's temperature and listened to her chest. She told the nurse she was calling Elise Wainwright, Andi's aunt, who could give them more medical history on her.

"Hi Kelly," said the bright voice on the other end. "What's up?"

"Elise, we're at the emergency room. It's Andi. She was feeling dizzy and then threw up."

"Oh, my God. What happened?"

"Well, at first, I thought it was a bug or something. She originally wanted me to take her home, but I decided to take her to urgent care. On the way, she started slurring her words and had trouble opening her eyes. That's why I brought her here. We just got here. I'm going to give the phone to the nurse as soon as she's ready for you. I thought you could give them more information on her medical history."

"Okay, I'm getting in the car and coming over there right now."

"I'd rather not have you in an adjoining room, so please be careful."

Kelly handed the phone to Andi's nurse. "This is Elise Wainwright, Andi's aunt. She can tell you more of her medical history than I can."

Kelly listened as the nurse asked Elise questions and typed her notes on the computer in the treatment room. A few minutes later, the nurse handed Kelly's phone back to her.

"Thanks. That was quick thinking. Are you related to the patient?"

"I'm her partner. We live together."

"All right. When did Andi start feeling sick?"

"I'm not sure. She seemed fine this morning before she went to work on her new art gallery downtown. I believe she was there in the shop alone today. I have a business renovating houses, so I was at work too."

"How did you find out she wasn't feeling well?"

"I got a call from her a little while ago saying she was feeling dizzy and sick and didn't think she could drive herself home." Kelly continued to explain the events that led up to her bringing Andi to the Emergency Room. "When Andi started slurring her words, I figured I'd better bring her here instead."

The nurse nodded. "I'd say you made the right decision. Is she on any medications?"

"No. None."

"I have to ask this next question. Is it possible she might've taken or eaten anything that caused this? What about any recreational-type..."

Kelly answered her before the nurse could finish asking her question. "No. Not a chance. That's not her at all. Andi won't take even an aspirin unless she must. She's gotten so wound up in work that she's forgotten to eat. However, I took her a mid-morning snack and we ate the same exact thing, so that can't be it. As I said, she was fine this morning. She seemed to think it came out of nowhere, and I can testify to that."

"Well, we'll run some tests and see what it is. Meantime, we'll get her on some IV medications to stop the nausea, so that should make her more comfortable. You're welcome to stay with her if you like. We'll be in and out, but for now she needs to stay awake. Can you keep talking to her?"

"I can do that. Do you have any idea yet what could be the problem?"

"She's not running a fever, so it's probably not an infection. It could be a migraine. We'll have a better picture of what's going on in a little bit. The doctor will be here soon and by then her aunt should be here too." The nurse patted Kelly's shoulder. "Don't worry, we'll take good care of her."

"Thank you. I know you will."

CHAPTER SEVEN

ELISE PRACTICALLY SPRINTED INTO the emergency room and straight to the front desk. The nurse sat up just a little straighter before Elise could even speak to her.

"Ms. Wainwright, we're expecting you. Your niece is in treatment room five. Marisa here will take you right back." The nurse indicated a young woman in scrubs standing next to her.

"Thank you," Elise said, nodding at her without slowing down. Marisa trotted off at a fast clip and Elise followed her through the double doors, scanning the treatment rooms for number five. Before she could find it, Marisa was pulling one of the sliding glass doors open and waving her in.

Elise paused at the door. Nothing could've prepared her for the sight of her niece lying there, pale and still in a room full of stainless steel and glass. Kelly was sitting at Andi's side holding her hand and whispering to her. Andi's eyes were closed, but she was nodding a little and appeared to be answering Kelly.

Kelly stood up when she saw Elise and stroked Andi's face to get her attention. "Andi, your aunt is here now. I'm going to let her hold your hand for a while, if that's all right. You need to keep talking and stay awake."

Andi nodded and opened her eyes somewhat, blinking as she answered, "Okay."

Elise reached to hold Andi's hand and sat in the chair next to Andi's bed. She looked up at Kelly and mouthed a 'thank you.'

"Aunt Elise, I'm sorry…" Andi's voice was soft, her words drawn out.

Elise let out a sigh. "Oh, my sweet girl. What in the world do you have to be sorry for? You didn't do anything except get sick. Don't worry, sweetheart, you're in good hands here."

Andi took a couple of breaths and licked her lips. "They're so nice…except they won't let me sleep."

"I'm sure they won't. Not without having a clearer picture of what's wrong with you. I imagine that's their standard procedure. I know you don't feel well, but for now you need to stay awake. I promise you can sleep later." As Elise stroked Andi's face, she flashed back to that same little girl Andi used to be, when she was sick from the flu. It was hard to see her sick at ten years old, and nearly as difficult to see her sick now. She glanced over at Kelly and smiled. Now Andi also had Kelly to take care of her. She felt herself relax a little as Kelly put her hand on her shoulder.

"I'll let you sit with her for a bit by yourself," Kelly whispered to her. "I think I'll go find something to drink and move my truck to the parking lot. Can I bring you anything from the cafeteria?"

"Actually, I could use a bottle of water." Elise stood up and put her arm around Kelly. "Thank you so much for being there for her. You've no idea what a comfort you are."

Kelly hugged Elise. "I love her too, you know. Of course, I'm here for her." She held Elise back and stared into her eyes. "And if you ever need me, I'll come running for you."

Elise smiled. "I bet you would. Thank you."

"I'm glad you know you can count on me. By the way, we're not supposed to let Andi fall asleep yet."

"I'm on the job." Elise sat back down and held Andi's hand again.

As Kelly walked out the door, Elise stroked Andi's forehead once more and asked, "Andrea, what happened? I talked to the nurse on the phone. I'd like to hear from you what happened, though, if you can tell me." She already knew what Kelly had told her on the phone, but hoped to keep Andi talking enough to keep her awake.

Andi's eyes opened partway, blinked, and then closed again as her lips curved into a little smile at her aunt. "I honestly have no idea," her voice barely above a whisper. "I was...fine this morning."

"When did you start feeling bad, then?" Elise stroked Andi's hair.

"After lunch, I think," Andi said, her words drawn out. Andi licked her lips again. "Can I have something to drink?"

"I'll go ask the nurse. Promise me you'll stay awake."

Andi nodded.

"I'll be right back." Elise let go of Andi's hand long enough to step to the treatment room door. As soon as she put her head out, the nurse was right there. "Can Andrea have something to drink? She's thirsty."

"I'll get her a swab or some ice chips for that. Her IV is rehydrating her, so the thirst should wear off soon." The nurse stepped into the room and patted Andi's foot. "Miss Andi, I need you to talk to me for a minute."

"Okay," Andi answered, squinting as she seemed to force her eyes open slightly.

"Can you tell me where you are?"

She blinked as she smiled, seeming to think about the answer for a few seconds. "Hmm...I've got that one. The hospital."

The nurse nodded at Elise. "That's right. Can you tell me what day of the week today is?"

"Um...I think Wednesday."

"Good girl. You're doing better."

Andi put her hand over her eyes appearing to try to shade them. "It's so bright in here."

"Yes, I know, and I'm sorry but that's how it usually is. We do have to see what we're doing. Tell you what, I'll turn the lights down a little for you." She reached for one of the switches. "How's that? Any better?"

"Thank you." Andi's words were still drawn out and slow. She blinked her eyes as the nurse turned off one set of lights over her bed. "That feels so much better."

"Does your head still hurt?" the nurse asked.

"Some. Not as bad as when I came in. Do you know yet what happened to me?"

"It's possible that you're having a migraine. Have you ever had one before?"

"Not that I know of. I don't...remember."

Elise shook her head. "I've never known her to have a migraine. As far as I know, she rarely gets any kind of headache."

"Well, Miss Andi, we ran an EKG and a CT scan. Although your heartbeat was a little erratic when you came in, it seems to be more normal now. The doctor should be back to see you in just a few minutes. She'll go over all the test results with you. Meantime, I'll get you something for your dry mouth."

A couple of minutes later, the nurse returned with a cup containing a small amount of water and a little sponge on what looked like a lollipop stick. She handed them to Elise. "She can swab her mouth with this as she needs it. That should make her feel better."

Kelly returned a minute or two later with two bottles of water, handing one to Elise. Elise stood up, offering the seat closest to Andi back to her. Kelly put her hand on Elise's shoulder. "You can stay right there if you like. We'll take turns."

A woman in scrubs and a white lab coat appeared at the door. "Hi, Miss Andi. I'm Dr. Carter." She patted Andi's foot, then looked up at Elise. "And you must be Elise Wainwright." She reached out to shake hands. "It's nice to meet you, although I'm sorry this had to happen under such uncomfortable circumstances."

"It's nice meeting you, although I'd rather it was under other circumstances, as well. And this is Andrea's partner, Kelly." Elise put her hand on Kelly's arm.

"Nice to meet you," Dr. Carter said to Kelly. "Now, let's see what we can do for our patient here." She walked to the other side of Andi's bed. "Miss Andi, I need you to sit up for a few minutes." She hit a switch, raising the head of the bed very slowly. The movement didn't seem to bother Andi so much as the effort to sit up and not topple over to one side. The doctor listened to Andi's chest for a bit in several spots, and then listened to her back, finally letting her sit back against the bed.

"All right, your chest sounds pretty good," Dr. Carter said, addressing her comments to Andi. "So, here's what we have. Although your heart and chest sound pretty good now, the tests we ran show that you've had a heart attack."

"But..." Andi began.

Dr. Carter interrupted her. "I know, you think you're too young for something like that, but it can happen. Have you been under a lot of stress lately?"

"I guess it's possible." Andi closed and then opened her eyes slowly. "My new art gallery downtown." She let out a long sigh. "Maybe I overdid it?"

Kelly and Elise nodded a silent yes in response.

"That could be. Is there a history of heart disease in your family?"

Elise spoke up. "Her mother died while giving birth to Andrea's little brother. They said it was related to her heart, but I don't know any more than that."

"It's entirely possible that you've inherited a bit of weakness in that direction. We'll keep you here tonight and depending on how you do, a couple more days for a few more tests. This way you get some rest, which I'm sure you realize you need. Meantime, we'll get you all set up for the rest of the tests and you can get some sleep. I'm sure you're exhausted. Once we get you upstairs, they'll bring you some dinner or we might let your aunt here or Kelly bring you something within reason." Dr. Carter looked at Kelly and Elise. "I think you'll find the food here's actually pretty good."

"I'll be fine with the hospital dinner." Andi put her hand out. "And thank you."

Dr. Carter shook Andi's hand with one hand, and then patted it with the other. "Oh, and if you think you're going to work while you're in here, think again. Rest means rest. These two are absolutely not allowed to bring any work to you." She looked pointedly at each one of them and then back at Andi. "Take some time off and rethink how you're going about your business, either getting some help or going slower. You've got to take better care of yourself."

Andi heaved a sigh. "I get it."

Dr. Carter pursed her lips. "I'm not sure you actually do, but you will. This is nothing to play around with. You could've been in big trouble. I'm glad we got you when we did."

"Kelly...she brought me in. I tried to get her to take me home."

Dr. Carter patted Kelly on the shoulder. "Well, then, Kelly, you probably saved her from having more damage to her heart. Good job."

"All I knew was that she needed more than urgent care. I'm glad she called me and didn't try to drive herself home. It looks like we both made some good decisions today." Kelly patted Andi's leg through the warming blanket.

"Okay, then, Miss Andi, we'll get you admitted and scheduled for some more tests, including an MRI. I'll see you upstairs later." She turned to Elise. "Again, nice to meet you, Ms. Wainwright. I can't tell you how much your donations and fundraising for that cardiac wing mean to us and to our patients."

"Please call me Elise. I was happy to do it. Who knew my own family might be using it someday."

Dr. Carter turned to Kelly. "Could I see you outside for just a minute?" When she saw Kelly's surprised look, she laughed. "Don't worry, you're not in trouble." She walked around the bed and patted Kelly on the arm as she led her outside the room.

CHAPTER EIGHT

ONCE THEY WERE OUTSIDE the treatment room door, Kelly asked, "Is there something I need to do?"

Dr. Carter put her hand on Kelly's shoulder. "Actually, I'm a little concerned for you. Are you feeling all right? You look a little pale."

"I'm good," she said, looking down at the floor and shifting from one foot to the other and back again.

"Listen, it wouldn't be at all unusual for the spouse or partner of someone who's had a heart attack or become suddenly very ill to feel sick themselves. At the least many start blaming themselves or wondering what else they could've done for the patient. Believe me, you did a great job deciding to bring her straight here."

"When she called me, she said she felt too sick to drive home and wanted me to come get her. I dropped what I was doing immediately and went to get her. I keep wondering if there was some sign ahead of time that I might've seen and not realized what I was seeing. Maybe I could've forced her somehow to slow down. She was so excited about that new venture that I didn't want to get in her way. I knew she was overdoing it but..."

Dr. Carter shook her head. "Look, it's hard to get someone to slow down when they're doing something they love, although sometimes we need to do exactly that. Don't blame yourself for what happened. I'm guessing this was going to happen sooner or later anyway, if she inherited a weakness in her heart from her mother. We'll be able to tell more after those tests tomorrow."

"I wish I knew. I wish I'd insisted that she slow down. She's been burning that proverbial candle from both ends for a while now. I figured she'd back off as soon as the new place was up and running. She has another one in New York, but she's trusting one of her employees with the day to day operations on that one right now." A little tear escaped from one of Kelly's eyes and was quickly wiped away.

"Hey, you need to remember that what you did today was the best possible thing you could've done. We'll wait till tomorrow for the rest of the tests we need to run so she can rest. I have a feeling she'll make a full recovery because of you. Stop trying to second guess yourself and continue to be there for her. This episode might've scared her enough to make her back off for a bit and let someone help her more."

Kelly let out a sigh. "I sure hope so. Thank you, Doctor."

"You're welcome." She reached into her jacket and pulled out a card and wrote something on the back. "This is my personal cell number. Don't hesitate to call me if you or Andi have any questions at all."

"Thank you." Kelly took the card and looked at it for a second, and then back at Dr. Carter. "Just out of curiosity, are you always this good to your patients?" She grinned. "I mean, this sure feels like special treatment."

She grinned back at her. "I try to be. I'll admit this is a special case."

"How's that?"

"Elise Wainwright has done so much for this hospital that we could never ever thank her enough. She's never been a patient here, so having the chance to do something above and beyond for her niece is the least we can do."

"Wow...I had no idea. Elise is a very special woman and a great friend. I keep finding out new things about how amazing she is."

Dr. Carter smiled. "Looks like you're involved with a pretty nice woman, yourself. Take care of her, and I'll see her tomorrow after her tests. Don't hesitate to call me any time if either of you has any questions or concerns." She reached to shake Kelly's hand before leaning into the room to say goodbye once more to Andi and Elise.

Kelly stood there for a minute longer, shoving the business card into her pocket as she watched Dr. Carter walk away. Knowing Andi and Elise were wealthy was one thing, but appreciating what they did with what they had was another thing altogether. She loved both of those Wainwright women. The thought of losing either of them was more than she wanted to contemplate. Swiping at her watering eyes again, she walked back into the treatment room.

Elise looked up as Kelly walked back into the room. "Do you mind if I ask what Dr. Carter wanted?"

"Not at all. She wanted to give me her card and tell me she's available any time we need her. That was nice, wasn't it?" Kelly sat in the other plastic chair next to Andi's bed. "She also said I might feel bad about Andi being sick and told me I did the best thing for her." She searched Elise's eyes. "I did, didn't I? I worried I might've seen this coming and not understood what I was looking at."

Elise reached for Kelly's hand and held it in hers. "Kelly, you probably saved her life. You thought fast and brought her here. There's no way you could've known Andrea had any kind of heart problem, since even I wasn't aware of it. She's always been very healthy and active. If she'd been sick or hurt I would've known about it, believe me."

Kelly let it out in a sigh. "Thank you for telling me. That was the other thing Dr. Carter wanted to talk to me about...feeling guilty. She said that's a common feeling. I hope you understand I'd never want anything to happen to either of you. You're both special to me."

"You're pretty special yourself. Now, don't beat yourself up over this, since no one saw it coming. Now that we're all aware of it, we can make sure Andrea doesn't get as stressed out in the future."

Kelly looked over at Andi, dozing in the hospital bed, and chuckled. "That should be fun. You know how she is."

Elise smiled back. "Yes, I do. By the way, I'd say it's looking like Friday's cookout is off. I'll tell Lauren and you need to tell your friends right away. Dr. Carter did say she could be in here for a few days."

Kelly nodded. "Andi has reservations to fly back to New York early Sunday morning. She said there were some things to take care of in person at the New York gallery. I don't know who to contact there, but she won't be able to do that, either."

Elise appeared to think for a few seconds. "True. Tell you what, since I have the gallery number, I'll call them. You should have that number too, for future use. I know you always call Andi's cell when she's up there, but, like today, you might need it. I'll text it to you after I call them."

Kelly stepped outside the treatment room again and called Shawn, who immediately wanted to come down to the emergency room. Kelly talked her out of it, since Andi's condition had settled down and she was sleeping until they could get her into a room.

"How about if Carrie and I go over to your house and take care of Piper for you? We can let her out and feed her. I'm sure she'd love to see Carrie anyway, since she'll probably bring over some of her special Piper food. That'd be one less thing for you to worry about today. How does that sound?"

"Thank you. I appreciate that and so would Piper, I'm sure. Tell Carrie thanks. I'll let you know what happens as soon as we know anything."

"That sounds great. And Kelly?"

"What?"

"Call us anytime if you or Andi need anything. And I do mean anything. Before we come tomorrow, we'll call first to see if Andi's up to company. If she is, then we'll see you tomorrow afternoon. Take care of yourself, buddy."

Kelly thanked Shawn again and ended the call just as the nurse came back into Andi's room. She roused Andi, checked her blood pressure, and listened to her chest again. "Miss Andi, there's a room ready for you upstairs. Transportation is on their way to take you up and should be here in a couple of minutes." She looked at Kelly and Elise. "You're welcome to walk up with her, if you'd like."

"We'd love to. Thank you," Elise said. She patted Andi's leg. "Looks like you're going to get lots of rest now."

CHAPTER NINE

IT WAS DARK WHEN Kelly finally left Andi at the hospital and drove home. She'd stopped beating herself up over what happened, but fear still sat hard in the pit of her belly. Just the thought of losing Andi after all they went through to be together made her stomach clench and her eyes water. She didn't cry. Yet, her eyes did water and she had to wipe those watery eyes several times as she drove. Must've been allergies.

She kept playing over in her head all the times that she'd thought about telling Andi how much she loved her. It never seemed to be exactly the right time or romantic setting that she imagined. It didn't happen the way Kelly thought it should, but she was glad she told Andi when she did. She knew it meant a lot to her to finally hear those words and now she wished she'd told her a whole lot sooner.

As Kelly walked through her front door, it struck her how empty the house felt, even as Piper jumped into her arms and covered her face with puppy kisses. When she and Piper had lived there alone while renovating that very house, it had seemed just fine. Once Andi moved in, the house seemed to fill with her presence, her warmth. Even the thought of what might've happened. Well, it didn't. She had to make herself stop thinking that way. Andi was going to be fine. She had to be.

"Good girl, Piper," she said, letting Piper down. "Let's look for a treat for you and one for me, okay?" Piper started prancing around as soon as she heard the word 'treat,' as always. Her phone went off, playing Shawn's familiar ringtone.

"We're calling to check on you," Shawn said, concern evident in her voice. "I'm sure Andi's being taken care of and we went over and fed Piper, but what about you? Did you eat?"

"I had something at the hospital cafeteria." Kelly put the phone on speaker as she walked into the kitchen, Piper following close at her heels to make sure her mommy didn't get lost on the way to the treat cabinet. Piper knew right where they were kept.

"Oh, boy, hospital food." Shawn's sarcasm was clear.

Kelly opened the kitchen cabinet and retrieved the plastic

container with the little steak-shaped dog treats in it. "It wasn't that bad, actually. I hadn't been in there in years and it has vastly improved since then." She put a few of the treats in Piper's food bowl and smiled as she watched her promptly devour each one.

"I imagine Andi is sleeping away for sure by now. How's Elise doing?" Shawn asked.

"Yes, Andi was sleeping when I left. As for Elise, I made her go home an hour ago. Lauren was going to meet her at the house and be with her for a while."

"Wow. That poor woman must be exhausted."

"Actually, she's got the stamina of a superhero. She didn't seem tired at all, even though she had to be. We were there all afternoon and well into this evening." Kelly paused to yawn. "I just walked in the door here at home and I'm pooped. You'd think I'd been doing heavy lifting all day."

"I'll bet. Look, if you need anything—anything at all—you know all you need to do is ask, right?"

Kelly smiled. "Yes, I do. You and Carrie are always there for me and I appreciate you coming over and feeding Piper. Thanks for turning on some lights. Coming home to a not-dark house was nice."

She opened the freezer door and took out the container of rocky road ice cream while she was chatting, reached for a spoon, and sat in the kitchen nook to take a few bites out of the carton.

"Oh, by the way, Andi is in room 463, which is a very nice private room. I had no idea they even had rooms like that in a hospital. It's on the new cardiac wing and feels more like a hotel room. And guess what...I found out while I was there that Elise had a lot to do with it being built. She donated a lot of money and raised funds for the rest. I understand the whole wing is like that."

"Wow. That's pretty amazing."

Kelly yawned. Just a little one. "Yeah, it is."

"Listen, I can tell you're tired, so I won't keep you. Like I said, if you need anything, don't hesitate to call us. We'll come to the hospital to visit Andi tomorrow after Carrie gets off work, if that's okay. We'll call you first to make sure she's up to visitors."

"That sounds like a plan. They're going to run some more tests on her tomorrow during the day, so that'd be great. And Shawn..."

"What?"

"Thank you for being my friend."

"Of course. Always."

Kelly ended the call, put the ice cream back in the freezer, and rinsed off the spoon before she tossed it into the dish drainer. Kicking off her shoes at the bottom of the stairs, she shuffled her way up to their bedroom. A few minutes later, she was undressed and lying on the bed with the TV on for company, flicking through channel after channel. Piper dragged her little blanket over and cuddled up to Kelly's side as she settled the blanket nest-like around herself. Kelly picked up her phone a couple of times and started to call the direct number to Andi's room, but stopped before she tapped the final number, not wanting to wake her if she was asleep. It was going to be a long night.

CHAPTER TEN

KELLY STUCK HER HEAD into Andi's hospital room to see if she was awake. "Good morning, sunshine! How's my favorite girl?"

Andi was propped up into a semi-sitting position and a grin lit up her face. "I bet Piper is fine." She chuckled as she reached for the bed remote and sat up a little more. "How are you? Did you get some sleep?"

"I've slept better. I bet you had it much worse than I did, though. Don't they usually wake you up ten times during the night to take your temperature or blood pressure or something?"

Andi grinned widely and held out her arms for a hug. "It wasn't that bad."

Kelly placed the little vase full of wildflowers on Andi's bedside table. She sat on the edge of the bed, folded Andi gently into her arms and held her, one hand slowly stroking her back. "I missed you so much. I always miss you when you're not home. I'm not used to sleeping by myself anymore." She kissed her tenderly before Andi's head nestled onto her shoulder and she whispered, "I do love you, you know."

"I know. I love you too. I've been pretty sure you loved me for a while now, but I especially needed to hear you say it yesterday. I want you to know that I'll never ever get tired of hearing you tell me you love me." Andi gave Kelly another little kiss, and sat back against her bed.

Kelly reached to caress the side of Andi's face. "I'm sorry I waited so long. I was sure you already knew, and that you were waiting to hear me say it. The thing is, I didn't want to simply tell you, I wanted to tell you in some special way. I wanted to take you somewhere romantic, like in one of Shawn's books. It turned out that in the truck on the way to the emergency room had to make do. That wasn't exactly romantic, and I'm sorry for that."

"Oh, honey, that was romantic enough for me. For some reason, I had to make sure you knew that I loved you right then. I wanted you to hear it from me, just in case. I was feeling pretty awful and I was scared I might not get another chance."

Kelly touched Andi's hand, turned it over, and kissed her palm. "I want you to know in your heart that I didn't tell you I loved you in the truck because I thought you wanted to hear me say it. I said those words because I do love you. I've loved you for a long time now. I guess I didn't know how to tell you."

Andi smiled. "I almost told you myself so many times. I thought it should come from you first because of what we've been through. I didn't want you to think I was rushing things even more. It was my idea to move in together because you were selling the house I wanted to live in. I didn't want to live there alone. I wanted to be with you there. Anyway, I decided to wait until you were ready."

"And you waited and waited." Kelly leaned forward to place another gentle kiss on Andi's lips. "You're a patient woman."

"And now I'm a patient." A little chuckle, then a little smile made its way to her eyes. "Okay, that's the funny for today. Sorry, I've never been great at jokes. Thanks for the pretty flowers. You didn't have to do that. I'm only going to be in here for another day or so."

"You're welcome. I thought they'd brighten up the room. Have they told you what's on the schedule for today?"

"I've already been down for my CT scan. They did that very early this morning."

"Why didn't you call me? I would've come to be with you."

"Why? There was nothing for you to do. They came and got me very early, as I said. Somebody must've come in before their shift or something, because they didn't let me eat or drink anything after the dinner they brought me last night. At least I've had some breakfast now. It did make me kind woozy for a bit, and I'm still tired. Did you eat?"

Kelly let go of Andi's hand and moved off the side of the bed onto the chair next to it. "I stopped for one of those biscuit things with eggs and sausage." Andi looked at her, eyebrows raised and head tilted in question. "Okay, I had two of them." Kelly laughed. "You know me too well now."

"At least you ate. Sweetie, you don't need to hang around here all day. You have work to do on the renovation and you'd only get antsy sitting around here all day with me. Besides, I think they're planning to do something else to me in a bit. I forgot what. I thought they said something about an MRI, although I don't remember now, to be honest."

"I know, but...well...I feel like I should be here with you." Kelly reached for Andi's hand again and absently stroked the back of it with her thumb. "You scared me."

Andi put her other hand over Kelly's. "I'm sorry about that."

"Who knows, this might've happened anyway, if it's a health problem you weren't even aware of." She reached to touch Andi's face as she looked into her eyes. "I'm so glad you're going to be okay. You've got nothing to feel sorry for, other than maybe working more than you should've been."

"I'm sorry about that. I shouldn't have gotten so wound up in this new venture. I shouldn't have been up all hours and I should've eaten better. Most of all, now that I'm thinking of it, I shouldn't have ignored you so much." Andi took a deep breath and let it out slowly. "I'm especially sorry about that."

"Look, this project is something you're passionate about. You couldn't help getting so excited and involved with it. Plus, we're both still sort of new at this relationship. I've never lived with anyone before, besides Piper I mean. I've never been in this situation. I feel like the world's tilting and if I'm not careful we'll fall off or something. That sounds crazy, doesn't it?"

"No, not at all. Look, we're finally making a life together and this had to happen. I'm feeling rather at odds with all this, but I'm going to be fine. Really. My mother died much younger than I am, and I probably don't have what she had, whatever that was. I'm not going to die. I promise."

Kelly felt her eyes start to well up and covered it by yawning, and then wiping at her eyes. "I'm going to hold you to that promise. I'm so sorry you lost your mother so young...and your dad, when he lost it after your mom died. Then again, you've had a good life growing up with Elise. She loves you so much that I'm sure she couldn't love you more if she'd given birth to you herself."

"I know she does. By the way, she called a bit before you got here. She'll be over in a while, so I won't be alone." Andi patted Kelly's hand. "Tell you what, if you want, you can sit here with me till Aunt Elise comes. Then you can go to work for a while. If you want to bring your lunch up here, I'll eat lunch with you. Does that make you feel better?"

"Some." Kelly smiled, let go of Andi's hand again and sat back in the chair. "This doesn't feel like some hospital bedside chair, that's for sure. It's comfortable. I remember this chair from last night." She ran her hands over the upholstered and stuffed chair arms. "Okay, it's very comfortable. This is quite a room you have here."

"It's actually a recliner. I didn't realize it until this morning. One of the aides here showed me how it worked so when I'm more ambulatory I can sit in it. All you have to do is lean back."

Kelly pushed back in the chair, causing a footrest to unfold from underneath. "Wow...nice." She stopped when it brought her legs up.

Andi grinned. "So, how is it? Still comfortable as a recliner?"

"Very." She ran her hands along the armrests again.

"See, now you can be all comfy while you're here."

Kelly tried to stifle another yawn. "Not too comfy. I don't want to go to sleep, even though this is very relaxing."

"Well, you can sit there and enjoy that chair while I use the bathroom. I called the nurse and she'll be here any minute."

Kelly sat back up. "I can help you."

Andi put her hand up in a stop motion. "No, the nurse has to do it. There's an alarm that screams bloody murder if I get out of my bed without one of them. A nurse or aide must come turn it off anyway. Speaking of..."

A nurse dressed in blue scrubs appeared at the doorway. "Miss Andi, what can I do for you? Ah, I see you have company."

"Another trip to the bathroom, please. Nurse Sarah, this is my partner, Kelly. She offered to help me, but I didn't want to set off that alarm. Again." Andi rolled her eyes and shook her head. "It wasn't pretty the last time. It sure was loud."

Sarah walked around the bed to Kelly and reached to shake hands with a "nice to meet you." Then she reached for a switch on the wall behind Andi's bed. "There you go. It's loud for a reason. We don't want our favorite patient to fall. Once we're sure you're able to walk there and back, we'll get rid of the alarm; until then you know the drill."

It took a couple of minutes for Andi to turn around on the side of the bed and gradually stand up holding onto Sarah's arm. Kelly watched from her chair and when Andi was safely into the bathroom, she leaned back into that cozy chair again. With all the quiet, she thought it might feel nice to lay her head back for just a minute. Within seconds her eyes were closed and she was out like a light.

When Andi came out of the bathroom, Elise was standing there with her finger to her lips in the "shush" position. She pointed to Kelly asleep in the bedside chair.

"Poor baby," Andi whispered. "She said she didn't sleep much last night. Looks like she was more tired than she thought. Let her sleep."

As Sarah helped Andi back into bed she whispered, "Okay, Miss Andi, I think the next time you need to get up you might be steady enough for us to take that alarm off your bed. You did well this time, but I don't think you're quite ready to walk by yourself yet. Let's not take any chances we don't have to."

"Okay. I'm all for being safe. By the way," she indicated Elise, "this is my aunt, Elise Wainwright."

Nurse Sarah finished tucking Andi back into bed before reaching her hand out to shake hands. "You're not the Elise Wainwright whose name I've seen on that plaque in the hall downstairs, are you?"

Elise grinned. "Yes, that's me. Believe me, that wasn't all my doing. A lot of other people had a hand in paying for this wing. I simply got the ball rolling and put it out there."

"And twisted some arms, from what I hear," Andi said. "You're quite good at some friendly arm twisting."

"What can I say? Everyone's good at something." Elise patted Andi's arm and looked at Sarah. "So, how's our girl doing today? Better?"

"She's doing very well. She might be allowed to go home tomorrow if she promises to rest. It depends on what today's tests show." She looked at Andi. "You, young lady, are lucky your partner there brought you straight in here."

Andi looked over at Kelly sleeping away in the chair and smiled. "Yeah. She's pretty special anyway."

"Yes, she is," Elise added.

CHAPTER ELEVEN

A COUPLE OF DAYS later, Kelly opened the passenger door of the Durango and reached to help Andi out. Andi took her hand, grinning as she shook her head.

"Good grief, I'm not an old woman who can't get out of the car. You just sprung me from the hospital, and I can walk by myself now."

"I know." Kelly grinned back. "I like helping you. Give me a few days, and I'll be back to letting you get out of the truck by yourself."

Andi pursed her lips and let out a sigh. "It'd better take less than that. Hovering over me won't make me feel any better. In fact, it makes me feel worse. One thing that will help me feel much better is having something good for supper." She indicated the door to the Blue Bayou Diner as she stepped out of the truck and let go of Kelly's hand.

"Right. Well, I thought having an early dinner would make it easier for you to take a nap when we get home. Anyway, since you seem to have enough energy, I'll let you walk without holding my hand or my arm." She closed the truck door and clicked the lock, tucking the keys in her cargo shorts pocket.

"I didn't say I don't want to hold your hand." Andi reached for Kelly's hand once again. "I said I didn't want you to think I had to hang onto you."

"Oh, I see. You want it to be your idea." She laughed. "Got it."

"Quit it. I'm looking forward to some real food. Hospital fare wasn't bad, but this is much more like it."

They walked the few yards to the door that Kelly held open for Andi. The smells of hamburgers and grilled onions greeted them, and Andi breathed in the delicious aromas deeply. "I'm fully aware this stuff isn't even close to what the doctor ordered. A little bit won't kill me though, and those aromas can't hurt me at all. I'll see if I can find something that I'm supposed to eat on their menu." Andi inhaled in a deep breath. "It sure smells heavenly in here."

The sign by the register near the door read 'seat yourself,' so they strolled down the length of the 1950's style counter until they found an empty booth next to the window. They slid into the blue vinyl-clad seats and reached for menus from the chrome holder next to the miniature jukebox on their table.

"Thanks for bringing me here. I feel better already." Andi grinned as she opened her menu.

"I thought you'd enjoy it, since we haven't been here in a while. You always seem to love it when we do come." Kelly continued to peruse her own menu.

"I do like it. We should come here more often."

Kelly looked over her menu at Andi. "Seems like we haven't been anywhere lately."

Andi put her menu down and looked back at Kelly. "True and I'm aware it's been often my fault. Like the doctor said, I need to slow down. I guess I'd better start taking better care of myself, not to mention taking better care of our relationship. I'm sorry I've been so preoccupied." She looked at Kelly pointedly. "And I will do better. I promise." She picked her menu back up. "There must be some healthier stuff in here somewhere."

"Tell you what, I'll try to eat healthier. I guess we could both do better."

"Eat what you want, honey. You don't need to order something other than your usual because of me. I'll find something. Believe me, simply being here feels great." Andi looked around the room. "I love this sort of kitschy décor. For some reason, it reminds me of that restaurant you took me to on our first actual date. Remember that?"

"You mean that pirate place? I don't remember now what it was called." Kelly grinned, then put her hand up like she was answering a question in class. "Oh wait, I remember now. Cockatoo Cove out at Fort Myers Beach. The waiter had a fake parrot on his shoulder and we had that grog stuff to drink. I remember having a great time there."

Andi grinned back and then sighed. "Yeah, it was fun. I remember thinking at the time how wonderful it was to be with someone who had such a playful sense of humor. That you were willing to take a date to someplace like that told me a lot about you." She leaned forward across the table and whispered, "I love you, Kelly Bradley."

"I love you right back, Andi Wainwright," Kelly whispered in return. Right then, she could've leaned forward a little bit more and kissed the lips attached to the face she loved. She didn't, and wouldn't, not there in a restaurant with people who could be watching. Later, however, she was definitely going to kiss those lips. A lot.

CHAPTER TWELVE

ELISE ANSWERED A KNOCK on the door to find Lauren standing there. "You don't need to knock now, as much as you're here." She stood aside. "Come on in."

"I don't usually, but I'm not here today at any of my usual times. I don't want to make you feel like I'm invading your privacy by barging in at all hours."

Elise looked at her. "You, my dear, will never be invading my privacy by being here. You should know by now that you're always welcome."

As soon as the door closed, Lauren gathered Elise into her arms for a kiss. "Mmm...now that was a nice welcome."

"And that was a nice hello." Elise smiled as Lauren released her. She turned to head for the kitchen with Lauren following.

"Just so you know, I don't plan to start showing up at all hours. I didn't get to come over this morning for coffee because of that call I told you about. Keeping up with office hours in Europe means very early overseas conference calls with a German client."

"Please. You're free to barge in any time you feel like it. So, what's up?"

"I wanted to see you, find out how Andi's doing, and how you're doing. I called the hospital, and they said she went home. Have you talked to her?"

Elise retrieved a bottle of Diet Coke for Lauren and returned to her spot in the breakfast nook where her iced tea awaited. She put Lauren's Diet Coke on the table and motioned for her to sit. "Yes, and she's tired, but okay. Not surprisingly, she didn't sleep that well in the hospital and was looking forward to being home and sleeping in her own bed."

Lauren slid into the bench across from Elise and picked up her soda. "I'm surprised they let her go home so soon. They only had her a short while." She tipped the bottle up for a sip, and then set it back on the table.

"I know. It surprised me too. They said her tests looked very good, and if she promised to rest until her next doctor's appointment, with absolutely no work, she could go home."

"I'll bet that's going to be hard for her. She's so much like you...sweet and hardheaded at the same time."

"Thanks. I think." Elise scrunched up her face into a rather lopsided questioning grin.

Lauren laughed. "That was a compliment. I'd also bet she's a lot like you were at that age. Working too hard and not eating or sleeping like she should all probably contributed to her winding up in the emergency room. Do you honestly think Andi's going to slow down? Or do you think that might've scared her a little?"

"It scared me, that's for sure. I wanted her to come here for her recovery, so I could keep an eye on her and Kelly could work. I even researched hiring a private nurse for her if she needed one. Kelly decided to stay home with her at least until her first outpatient visit. I can't make Andrea slow down, but I hope Kelly can convince her she has something more to live for than that new gallery."

"I bet. Kelly has a positive effect on the people she's close to. That's simply her nature. She's such a sweetie." Lauren sipped from her Diet Coke.

"Yes, she is. I'm so glad she and Andrea finally got together. They seem perfect for each other."

"Speaking of...I think we're perfect for each other." Lauren put her soda down. "I must admit that I do like cuddling with you." She grinned.

Elise blushed. "I like cuddling with you too." She stood up. "Speaking of...come with me. I want to show you something."

Elise held Lauren's hand and led her through the kitchen and down the hall. They paused in front of Elise's bedroom doors before Elise pushed open the door. She let go of Lauren's hand as she took the few steps to her closet and paused in front of the first dresser inside.

"I'm thinking it's time you stopped dragging an overnight bag back and forth." She opened the top drawer, showing that it was empty. "This one's yours if you'd like to keep some things here." She took a couple of steps farther and pointed out a cleared section of the closet. This is for you. What do you think?"

Lauren wrapped her arms around Elise and pulled her close. "What a nice surprise! I think that's a great idea. Thank you." Lauren put a finger under Elise's chin, turned her face up, and placed a sweet kiss on her lips. "I guess that might make it less obvious to the neighbors that I'm coming over to spend the night, wouldn't it?"

Elise pulled back slightly. "That's not why I did it. I don't care what the neighbors think. I thought that it'd make it nicer for you. Plus, we don't need to plan for you to be here overnight. If you want to stay, you can just stay."

"Very true. And very thoughtful of you. Thank you again."

"There's more." Elise stepped back, grasped Lauren's hand again, and led her back across the bedroom and into the bathroom. She opened the medicine cabinet. "I made some space in here for you. You know, for whatever you need."

"This is all very sweet of you...and quite a big step. I'm happy you want to do it, but I'm curious what brought this on?"

"Come sit with me out on the patio." She led her to the little walled patio outside her bedroom sliding glass doors, where they sat in the two chairs. "We've been together for a while now and I thought about how much I enjoy being with you. I'm not ready...and I might never be ready...to live with someone else. I'm awfully set in my ways."

"We both are. I understand what you're saying. I like my home and I'm not ready to give that up, either, as much as I love being here with you."

Elise nodded. "Still, there's no reason you can't be comfortable when you're here. I like having you around now, so I keep Diet Coke and a few other things in the fridge for you. I want you to feel like you can come over or stay overnight whenever we both want, without feeling like you must always keep a bag packed in your trunk or the like. That seems pretty silly."

Lauren gave her a little smile as she waved her hand dismissively. "I honestly don't mind."

"I know you don't, and that makes you even sweeter. So, what do you say? Want to bring some things over to leave here? How about a bathing suit?"

Lauren brought Elise's hand to her lips and kissed her fingers. "I'll bring some things over tonight." She put her arms around her waist. "I'm completely blown away. I didn't expect this."

"I thought it was one more step we could take to be closer." Elise gazed into her eyes. "We've decided not to rush anything. However, I want you to know how much I care about you and how much I want to keep you in my life."

"My dear, you're never going to be out of my life, if I can help it. I care for you very much and I want you to be happy. I love our cuddle nights. One day, there could be more for us, but I'm not in any hurry and hope you never feel rushed into anything."

"I don't. Your patience is one of the things I love about you. I hope you'll continue to be as understanding and considerate as you've been with me so far."

"Of course I will. I can't imagine what would make you think I might not. Sweetheart, I—"

She was interrupted by the chimes from the front doorbell.

Elise jumped up and let go of Lauren's hand. "I'll be right back. Don't go away."

Lauren chuckled and slumped back into the lounge chair as Elise headed for the front door.

A few minutes later, Elise returned to her bedroom patio. "Girl Scout cook—" There was Lauren, out like a light, her arms on the armrests and her head lolled to one side. *Poor baby. She must've been up quite early for that business call this morning.* She touched Lauren's shoulder lightly and whispered, "Come lie on the bed and take a little nap. You'll feel much better there than out here."

Lauren's eyelids fluttered, opening as she sat up. "I'm sorry, I didn't mean to fall asleep on you. I think I'll take you up on that nap, but only if you lie down with me." She reached for Elise's offered hand and got up slowly. "I can't believe I fell asleep like that."

Elise led Lauren to the bed. She pulled the pillows from under the bedcovers and fluffed them. "Come on, I'll lie down with you. At least until you fall asleep. How's that? Do you need me to wake you up at a certain time? Is there a meeting you need to go to?"

"My phone has an alarm on it. Let me look now before I fall asleep again." She retrieved her phone from her pocket and did a few quick flicks and taps. "I'm good for at least an hour. Then I need to get back to the office to prepare to meet some new clients. Never good to be late for your first meeting." She set the phone on the nightstand.

"No, it's not. Okay then, I'll be sure you're awake even if you sleep through your phone alarm." She patted the bed. "Come on, lie down."

Lauren sat down on the bed and without a word, Elise slipped Lauren's loafers off. Lauren laid down and put her arm out, waiting for Elise to come to the other side of the bed to lie down next to her. Elise cuddled into Lauren's shoulder, and within a couple of minutes heard Lauren's breathing slow to a familiar sleeping cadence. She smiled as she lay there in her favorite spot with Lauren's arm around her, inhaling her fragrance and listening to her breathe.

A few minutes later, Elise gently moved Lauren's arm and sat up very slowly. When she reached the bedroom door, she turned and gazed at Lauren lying there on her bed sleeping, and smiled again. She barefooted it out of the room and pulled the door closed with a nearly silent click.

CHAPTER THIRTEEN

"SO, WHEN ARE YOU going to tell us the name of your new gallery? We keep looking for an announcement in the News-Press about a grand opening." Shawn and Carrie were sharing one of the two facing loveseats in front of the fireplace in Kelly and Andi's living room. Andi and Kelly shared the other one. Shawn set her soda on the coffee table. "We're not after you to get back to work soon, that's for sure. We assumed by now it has a name, at least in your head."

"There is something running around in my head," Andi said. "Actually, I've come up with a couple of good ideas. I'm going to have to make a final decision soon because I also need to get a sign put up well before I open. Of course, there are also business cards, stationery, and interior signs, not to mention item tags to design and get printed."

Kelly put her arm around Andi and began lightly stroking Andi's arm. "Honey, you've got plenty of time to deal with all that. Right now, though, you're supposed to be resting."

"I'm sorry, my bad. I shouldn't have brought it up." Shawn looked pointedly at Kelly. "I wasn't thinking."

Andi waved them off. "Don't worry about it. It was nice of you to ask anyway. I'm still thinking about it some, even if I can't do anything about it."

"So, how are you doing now? Feeling any better yet?" Carrie asked.

"Some. I wish I didn't feel so blasted tired all the time." Andi shrugged. "I want this over with. I'm not a very patient person, I guess."

Kelly rolled her eyes and nodded.

"Ah. An impatient patient!" Shawn chuckled, making them all groan and smile at the same time. "When do you see the doctor again? Did she say to expect to feel like this?"

"I'll be seeing Dr. Carter the day after tomorrow in the afternoon. I'll ask her about it then."

Kelly reached for her soda. "Believe it or not, Dr. Carter gave me her personal cell number and said to call her any time."

Carrie sat upright. "Wow! I don't think I've ever heard of that happening before." She looked at Kelly and then at Andi. "You guys must be special. Have you called her yet?"

"No, we haven't done that. It's only been a few days since she got out of the hospital, so we assumed she'd be tired. That was quite an ordeal for anybody. Dr. Carter said she was to rest for a week and not do any work. Especially nothing stressful. We're trying to obey the doctor's orders."

"We, huh?" Carrie grinned. "So, you're keeping an eye on her?"

Andi groaned and turned to stare at Kelly. "Yes, she is. Kelly hasn't been back to work since I came home."

Kelly shrugged. "Well, what if you needed something and…"

Andi interrupted her. "I'm perfectly capable of hitting the little 'send' button on my phone that calls you. I'm not an invalid you know."

"No, you're not. I'm sorry if I made you feel like you were." Kelly pulled Andi a little closer, her hand returned to stroking up and down Andi's arm. "I only want to take care of you."

"I get that, honey. I do." She looked over at Kelly and patted her leg. "I wish you wouldn't worry about me so much."

Kelly kissed Andi's forehead. "I can't help it. Okay, I'll go back to work after your appointment with Dr. Carter, if she says you're good to be home on your own and I'm convinced you'll continue to rest. I guess I'm worried that you won't if I'm not here."

She snuggled up closer to Kelly. "You're probably right. Honey, it's not that I don't want you around. Your hovering makes me feel like an invalid. I'm not made of porcelain."

Kelly rolled her eyes as she smiled. "Okay. I'm sorry. I'll try not to hover. How's that?"

"Better. Carrie? Shawn? You two heard that, right? She's going to try not to hover. Let's see how long that lasts."

Shawn chuckled. "Aww, come on. You know she means well. Tell you what, Kelly, if I get sick you can come over and hover all you like. How's that?"

"Hey! That's my job!" Carrie smacked Shawn playfully on her arm. "I can hover."

"No, you can't. It's not your style." Shawn laughed. "Remember last fall when I got the flu? You set me up on the bed with the TV remote, a little cooler with bottles of water, and my phone. You put my laptop on the other side of the bed in case I felt like working. Then you went off to work. No hovering."

They all laughed.

Carrie shook her head. "Oh, come on, I was only a few minutes away in case you needed me. Anyway, you weren't that sick."

"Yes, I was. Okay, I thought I was. I had a fever, after all. Anyway, I slept a lot and I'm sure that was good for me. You weren't there. Maybe I should've called Kelly." Shawn was grinning.

"Good grief. Your fever was something like ninety-nine point two." Carrie looked at Andi. "See what I live with?" She patted Shawn's arm and gave her a little kiss. "I love you to pieces, honey, but you can be a baby when you're sick."

Andi laughed. "So far, Kelly hasn't been sick. I'm thinking it'll be payback time when it happens. I'll hover like crazy."

Kelly grinned. "What if I like it? I'll be spoiled silly and you'll be stuck with me."

"Then I'll call Shawn and get her to come over and take care of you. That'll cure you of that."

Kelly laughed. "Yeah, probably. She's not a good nurse and never has been."

Carrie raised her hand. "I can testify to that. She can't stand even the sound of someone throwing up or she needs to get away. We all have our weaknesses, and that's one of hers. So, Kelly, if you get sick don't bother calling Shawn unless you need a ride to the emergency room and Andi's out of town."

Kelly put her hand up. "All right. I'm going to let you all in on a little secret, speaking of hovering. The only reason Andi isn't at Elise's right now is because I'm here taking care of her. Elise was going to insist that Andi come to her house so she could take care of her. Elise still has her spare room set up for guests, and Elise said we could both stay with her until the doc released Andi to go back to work."

Andi drew back, looking Kelly in the eyes. "Really? I had no idea."

Kelly nodded. "Really. You scared the bejeezus out of her and me. Elise wanted to be sure you were well cared for. I bet she was going to hover worse than I am. Heck, she was talking about hiring a private nurse if you needed one."

Andi nodded her head slowly. "Good grief. That does sound like Aunt Elise. She does like to make sure I'm taken care of."

"Yeah, talk about hovering." Kelly raised her eyebrows as she asked, "How'd you like a private duty nurse hanging around all the time? You could have your very own Nurse Ratchett."

"Okay, okay." Andi threw up her hands. "I guess having you hanging around beats that alternative." She grinned and leaned against

Kelly again. "At least I can cuddle with you."

Kelly put her arm back around Andi and kissed the side of her head. "True."

Shawn laughed. "Hey, would you two like us to leave now?"

"No, no..." Kelly pulled Andi closer and then grinned. "Well, maybe..."

Carrie stood up. "It's time for us to go anyway. We just wanted to see how you're doing, Andi. It appears you're much better. If there's anything you need, give one of us a call, okay?"

Andi nodded.

"Yeah, keep up the good work." Shawn stood up and put her arm around Carrie's shoulders. She whispered loudly to Andi and Kelly, "And don't believe any of that stuff about what a baby I was when I was sick. I'm sure it was just a good story."

"Was not." Carrie laughed. "Anyway, if you'd like to get away and need us to take care of Piper, all you have to do is ask. She wouldn't mind staying with us. Maybe you could use a weekend somewhere. After the doctor approves, of course."

"That's a very nice offer, thank you." Andi looked at Kelly. "There's no reason we couldn't actually have a little vacation, right? We haven't taken one together yet."

"No, we haven't. You've been gone a lot to take care of your SoHo store, and when you're here, you're working away on the new one. I've been busy on this new house I'm working on. It would be nice to reconnect and relax." She looked at Carrie and smiled. "Thanks for the offer, Carrie. We might take you up on that sometime."

CHAPTER FOURTEEN

ELISE TRAILED ONE HAND in the warm water, lying on her stomach as she floated around her pool on a raft. Sunset was such a lovely time to relax. Crickets chirped from the yard beyond the pool cage as a breeze rustled the palm fronds and magnolia leaves in the trees. The little lights around the edge of the pool were the only illumination other than the swiftly dying sun. Still warm from the day, although not hot. Peaceful. Yes, very peaceful.

The sliding doors from the lanai opened and closed softly. There was a splash as Lauren dove into the pool and swam up to Elise's raft.

"Did I wake you up?" Lauren laughed as she shook her wet hair, spraying even more water on Elise.

Elise also laughed as she pulled Lauren onto the large raft. "I wasn't sleeping. I was just enjoying the evening. That is, I was until you decided to drench me."

"You're lucky I didn't yank you off that raft and—"

Lauren's threat was interrupted by Elise's lips on hers. "Still want to threaten me?"

"Um...maybe not. More like proposition you." Lauren let out a huge sigh. "You feel so good to me." She ran her hand over Elise's side, down toward her hip.

"Mmm...that feels nice, but don't get carried away. I'm..." Elise was interrupted by her cell ringing. It was on a small table, poolside. "I better get that. It's one of the girls." She rolled off the floatie and swam to the side of the pool, where she made short work of pulling herself up and onto the deck. She sat down on the lounge chair as she grabbed a towel and the phone at the same time.

"Elise, this is Kelly. I had to take Andi back to the hospital. We're in the emergency room again. We just got here."

Elise's breath caught and her stomach rolled over before she could answer, "What happened?"

"I'll explain more when you get here, but she was having similar symptoms to the last time."

"I'll be there as fast as I can. I was in the pool, so let me get dried off and dressed and I'll be on my way. Thanks, Kelly."

Elise ended the call and jumped up from the lounger. "It's Andi. They're at the ER again. I have to go."

Lauren was off the floatie like a shot. "I'm coming with you."

CHAPTER FIFTEEN

"WHAT HAPPENED?" ELISE ASKED Andi after giving her a kiss on her forehead and hugging Kelly. "I thought you were doing better." She sat in the chair next to Andi's bed and held her hand. The quiet was interrupted only by the sounds of beeping and clicking as the monitors hooked up to Andi's body went about their business.

"I...was...I..." Andi started, then seemed too tired to talk.

Kelly put her arm around Elise. "She was doing better. She was supposed to see Dr. Carter tomorrow afternoon. Instead, it looks like Dr. Carter will be seeing her tonight in here. I called her right before I put Andi in the car, and she should be here any minute. Meantime, she apparently called the ER and gave some orders, because they already knew Andi was coming before we got here."

"That was a good thing. At least you didn't need to start all over again and explain things to another doctor."

"No, we didn't. Besides, it's only been a week or so since she was here, so the last tests are very recent. They'll have something on file to compare the new ones to."

"True." Elise turned to Andi again and stroked her hair. "Sweetheart, how are you feeling now?"

"Not...so...great." Her words were slurred into each other. "So...tired."

"I know, I know." Elise picked up Andi's hand and put a little kiss on the back of it while she continued to hold it. She could feel a little tear forming in one eye and reached up to wipe it away with her free hand before it was noticeable.

"Honey, you're not supposed to go to sleep yet," Kelly said, patting Andi's leg through the blanket.

"I should go out to the waiting room and look for Lauren. She drove me here and dropped me off at the emergency entrance. She went to park her car, so she's probably out in the waiting room by now, looking for me." Elise turned to Kelly and started to get up. "I'll be right back."

Kelly sat Elise back down with a gentle push on her shoulder. "It's okay, I'll go. I've been hovering over Andi for days now and I think she might rather it was you for a bit. I need to walk around a little anyway. All you need to do is what we did last time. Keep her awake until the doctor gets here."

Elise held Andi's hand with one hand and with the other touched her own forehead in a little military salute. "I'm on the job." She reached to touch Kelly's hand. "Thank you."

Kelly smiled back and squeezed her shoulder in response, then disappeared out the door seconds later.

Elise gently stroked Andi's hand. "Andrea, you sure got a winner with your Kelly."

A faint smile. "Yes, I did."

"I guess I should've said 'our' Kelly. She was mine first, you know." Another little smile. "Mine...now."

"Yes, she is. I'm so glad you two finally got together. She's so good for you. She loves you very much."

"She told me. Love...her...too." Andi's words were drawn out, like she was making a real effort to talk. She appeared to struggle to focus her eyes on Elise. "Love...you...so much."

"I know, sweetie. I know. That's one thing I certainly would never doubt. I love you too."

"Aunt Elise..."

"What? Can I get you something?"

Andi's chest rose and fell as she slowly breathed in and let it out. "Lauren..."

Elise leaned in a bit to hear her. "What about Lauren?"

"She...cares...for you."

Elise smiled. "I know. I care for her very much."

"Don't...let...her..."

"Don't let her...what?"

"Get away." Andi seemed to manage a little smile. "Learn...from...my mistakes."

"Right. You're so much more mature than I am." Elise grinned and stroked Andi's hair.

Andi took another deep breath, holding on tighter to Elise's hand. "You've...pushed others away. Give her a chance. She could be...the one."

Elise put her other hand on Andi's as she sighed. "Andrea, sometimes I think you're trying to mother me."

"I'm...right about this."

"Maybe."

"Let her in."

A voice at the door said, "Let who in?" Elise looked up to see Lauren and Kelly standing there. Lauren had asked the question.

"You two, I guess." Elise got up and Kelly returned to sit next to Andi. Elise went to Lauren, who put her arm around her.

Kelly stroked Andi's face to get her attention. "I'm back. How are you doing?"

She opened her eyes slightly. "Hi, honey. I'm so tired."

"I'm sure you are. Just hang in there."

Elise asked, "I wonder what's keeping Dr. Carter?"

"She's coming. Since it was going to take her a while to get here, the ER had a Dr. Hill take a look at Andi when she got here. Dr. Hill has already talked to Dr. Carter and will call her back with what he finds. Looks like Andi here is very popular."

"Yes, she is very popular." Dr. Carter laughed as she strode in the door. "So, Andi, you must love our emergency room quite a bit to want to come back so soon. You couldn't wait till tomorrow to see me?"

Andi managed a little smile. "Yeah. That's it."

"Okay, then, let me check a few things and then we'll talk. I'll be right back." Dr. Carter patted Andi's blanketed leg and stepped out of the room, where a nurse handed her a tablet. They could see her scrolling through some entries, quickly through some, stopping to look at a few others longer. She nodded and said something to the nurse, then stepped back into the room.

"Well, Miss Andi, your blood tests show that you've had another little heart attack. You've earned yourself another stay here. We're going to keep a close eye on you and run a few more tests."

"Oh no, not again." Andi groaned as her body seemed to go limp "I can't...believe it."

"I'm sorry, I'm sure that's not what you wanted to hear. To put it bluntly, we don't know what's causing your problem and until we do, we can't take any chances on it happening again at home. Right now, I need to sit you up a bit so I can listen to your chest." Dr. Carter hit the button to move the head of the bed up, very slowly. As before, she had Andi lean forward so she could put the stethoscope to her back and listen, then lean back again so she could listen to her chest.

"Well, your chest sounds pretty good now. Your heartbeat is nice and regular. However, as I said, we're not taking any chances. We're not letting you out of the hospital this time until we are sure what's causing your problems. These two incidents were quite close together. Something is triggering them, and we need to find out what that something is."

"Okay, Doctor." Andi reached for Kelly's hand and held it hard, as she started to tear up. "I'm scared."

Dr. Carter reached for Andi's other hand and held it in both of hers as she looked directly into her eyes. "Andi, you're in the best possible place to be taken care of. We'll have you monitored so that if anything even starts to happen, we're going to be right here. Don't worry, we've got you." She turned to look at Elise and Kelly, smiling at them, and then back at Andi. "Thanks to your aunt here, we've got state of the art facilities and believe me, you're going to be watched the whole time."

"All right." Andi's voice wavered, apparently still close to tears as she spoke. "I trust you."

Kelly patted Andi's hand, looking up at Dr. Carter. "Thank you. I know you're going to figure this out."

Elise's hand had been on Andi's leg the whole time Dr. Carter spoke. Her hand absently stroked Andi's leg through the blanket. She couldn't help the tear that tried to escape, swiping it away quickly.

CHAPTER SIXTEEN

"MISS ANDI, I HAVE some news for you. We finally found out what caused your heart attacks." Dr. Carter sat in the second chair near Andi's bed, next to Kelly.

"Really? What?" Andi sat up a little straighter in her hospital bed.

"We discovered it with that angiogram we did this morning. Your problem is called SCAD, for Spontaneous Coronary Artery Dissection. It's quite rare. Despite this, at least we did find it."

"I've never heard of it, that's for sure. What is SCAD?" Kelly asked.

"It's easier to show you what it looks like." Dr. Carter took a tablet out of her coat pocket, poking and flicking at the screen until she found what she was looking for. "Here you go." She turned it around for them to see an illustration. "It's a tear in the inner wall of one of your coronary arteries. See this?" She pointed at it and then looked at them as they nodded. "It makes a little flap that allows blood to pool between the inner and outer walls of the artery and can form a clot. That clot can slow or even stop blood flow to your heart."

"What caused it? Did I do something?" Andi continued to stare at the image on the tablet.

"No one knows for sure what causes SCAD. So far, there are some indicators, but that's it."

"But I'm not old and I'm healthy. I don't even have high blood pressure. All right, I'm sure I haven't been eating right lately and I've been working very long hours, although I can't imagine how that would've done it."

Dr. Carter nodded as she hit a button and stuck the tablet back in her jacket pocket. "I understand your misgivings about this. Believe it or not, most cases involve otherwise healthy-appearing women about your age. The average age for this is about forty-two, just a little older than you are. According to your records, you've never had a baby. Correct?"

"Right."

"I understand your mother died from heart complications from giving birth to your younger sibling. Do you remember ever hearing what her heart problem was?"

"No, I was very young. My aunt said she never heard exactly what the cause was, only that it was related to her heart. No one knew she had any problems either. She had me without any complications, from what I understand. It happened when my little brother came along when I was about five. He died not long after my mother did."

"Just to rule things out, I'm recommending some genetic testing. Although it seems that you would've had other symptoms before now, sometimes patients with certain connective tissue disorders have had SCAD episodes. Your blood pressure is normal, so that isn't the cause. You've never used any drugs either? Like cocaine?"

Andi sat back and crossed her arms. "Hell, no! I'm not that stupid and besides, Aunt Elise would've killed me." She shook her head. "Those seem like odd questions, and I'm pretty sure they were in my file."

"Sorry, I had to be sure. According to your records, you've never had a stroke. Like I said, we don't have a definitive answer for what causes it, although some of those things have been associated with it."

"Okay, I understand. Now what?"

"I'm sure you're not going to like this, but I need to keep you in here for about a week. Rest is very important right now. It turns out that there are a couple of things we can do about it. We could go in and put a stent in that spot, however it seems that conservative, non-invasive treatment is often the best course. In your case, it's a tiny tear. We'll watch it and there's a good chance it'll heal up on its own. You'll be staying here longer this time—at least five to seven more days, as I said so we can keep an eye on you."

Andi let out a deep sigh. "You're right, I'm not excited about another hospital stay, but I understand."

Dr. Carter tilted her head as she looked closely at Andi. "Is there anything you'd like to ask me or are you feeling overwhelmed right now?"

Andi took a deep breath, blowing out her cheeks a bit as she let it out. "I think I'm a bit overwhelmed. I've never heard of this, and it's scary to think about. I do want to ask you one thing now, and please be straight with me." She reached for Kelly's hand and grasped it hard.

Dr. Carter nodded. "Okay, shoot."

"Can this happen again? I mean, I've had two heart attacks now, close together." Andi looked over at Kelly and back at the doctor. "How worried do I need to be about it?"

"I'm going to be completely honest with you and tell you that we don't know. It apparently can happen again. It could be years from now or never, we just don't know. What I can tell you is that you can't live the rest of your life losing sleep over this, thinking that it could happen again any minute. We're going to understand more about your situation in a few days. In your case, there was only one tear and apparently it caused both episodes. Once that one heals up, then maybe we'll get a better idea about your condition."

"It's still scary but at least we get what's causing the heart attacks, even if we don't have a clue how it got started." Andi squeezed Kelly's hand.

"True. Anyway, while you're here your job is to rest and let it heal as much as it can. After you're released, you'll need some cardio rehab, and after that you can go back to your normal life...if you stop trying to be three people in one. I want you to promise to get some help with that art gallery of yours."

Andi raised her hand. "I promise." She looked back and forth between Dr. Carter and Kelly. "Really, I do promise."

Kelly let go of Andi's hand and put her arm around her. "I'm a witness to that and will hold you to it. I'd like to keep you around for a very long time."

CHAPTER SEVENTEEN

"HOW'S THE HOSPITAL'S FAVORITE patient today?" Shawn asked as she and Carrie walked into Andi's hospital room.

Andi smiled as she released a long sigh. "I'm already tired of being hooked up to monitors and ready to go home any minute."

"Really? They're going to let you go home?" Carrie asked as they sat in the visitors' chairs. "It's only been a few days."

"No, not for a few more days." She heaved a sigh. "But I'm ready whenever they decide to let me leave. I guess I shouldn't have complained about Kelly's hovering."

Shawn laughed. "Yeah, I guess this is much worse, isn't it? Speaking of hovering, I'm surprised your aunt isn't here. She's been here every other time we were. Is she all right?"

"She's fine. They send her home when I'm supposed to be napping."

Carrie started to stand up. "Oh, no. We're not keeping you from—"

Andi waved her hand dismissively and motioned for her to sit back down. "Not at all. Seriously, I think I've more than caught up on sleep for a while. She'll be back shortly. Kelly should also be back up here soon."

"So...they both spend the whole evening with you?"

"Pretty much. I don't need to be babysat though." She leaned back and fiddled with her blanket. "I worry that Aunt Elise could be wearing herself out. I wish she'd just come to visit me during the day and go home. I'd rather she spent her evenings with Lauren. The thing is, I don't know how to tell her that without upsetting her."

Kelly came walking through the open doorway. She leaned over to give Andi a kiss, then sat on the side of her bed and asked, "Who are you trying not to upset?"

"Aunt Elise."

"Oh. Yeah. She's such a caring, loving woman. She worries about you a lot." Kelly reached for Andi's hand and held it.

"She does." Andi let it out in a sigh. "I wish she wouldn't, because then I worry about her. She's here at the hospital with me at all hours. The nurse sent her home, or she'd be here right now. She's in great shape, however, she's not in her forties anymore."

Carrie spoke up. "No, she isn't. She's probably in the best shape I've seen for someone in her mid-sixties but that's still no kid. Then again, none of the rest of us are." Carrie reached over and patted Andi's leg. "I've known Elise for several years now, and when she figures out what she wants, she goes after it. I'm sure if you talk to your nurse, she'll keep an eye out and send Elise home if it looks like she's had enough."

"I think maybe there's more to this than that," Shawn said, leaning forward with her elbows on her knees, her chin in her hands. "Do you two get to spend any time together? I mean, as together as can be in the hospital. You both had a scare, and I'm sure you could use some time alone."

Andi shook her head. "No, but we could. It feels like someone else is almost always around." She laughed. "No, I'm not telling you two to leave. At least not for a bit. It's nice of you guys to visit, and I'm enjoying your company."

"We can take a hint." Shawn stood up. "Tell you what. If you'd like, we can run over to your house and feed Piper this evening." She snapped her fingers. "In fact, I have an even better idea. How about we take her home with us, just until Andi comes home? She already has a bed there. We promise to feed her some actual dog food, not only Carrie's special treats. We can bring her back home as soon as Andi's sprung. Or we could return her sooner if you miss her too much. Either way, we'll make sure she's fed and taken care of. That'd be one less thing for you to be concerned about."

Kelly smiled. "Thanks, that would be nice of you. I'm sure Piper will appreciate not being left alone again all evening. She enjoys spending time at your house, so she most likely won't miss us much."

Carrie stood up. "Well, the feeling is mutual, that's for sure. We love her too. Shawn is home working even when I'm away at the office, so Piper will be better than fine. Now maybe you can convince Elise to go home earlier and you two can have dinner and the evening together here. Maybe you could even get some take-out instead of the hospital food."

Kelly nodded. "That sounds like a great idea. I guess we'll see what happens. Maybe I should call Lauren and ask her to talk to Elise. She might be able to convince her to go somewhere else for the evening.

That might work."

Carrie leaned over the bed and gave Andi a gentle hug. "If you need anything, call us. We'll go get Piper and see you tomorrow then."

"Thank you, Carrie. You and Shawn have been right here for us. We appreciate it."

"We do appreciate it very much." Kelly got up and hugged each of them. "Thank you. Both of you."

Shawn just smiled. "Nothing you wouldn't do for us. You've come to our rescue a few times."

Carrie patted Andi's leg. "That's what friends do. We'll go pick up my favorite four-legged little girl and head home to let the spoiling...I mean babysitting begin. Maybe you'll squeeze in a little time together before the next round of visitors comes around. I should warn you though, I might have a hard time giving Piper back."

Kelly grinned. "I'm more worried she might not want to come home after you've been pampering her."

CHAPTER EIGHTEEN

THAT SAME AFTERNOON FOUND Elise sitting at the glass-topped white wicker table on her lanai, her laptop on the table in front of her and a glass of iced tea at hand. She slid her finger up the screen or flicked at it with her left hand while her right absently reached for the glass for a sip. She looked up when she saw Lauren slide open the palm-etched sliding glass doors from the house to the lanai, Diet Coke bottle in hand.

"Hi there. I didn't think I'd see you this time of day. What's up?"

"Just checking on you again. You seem deep in thought." Lauren sat down in the chair next to Elise, placing her soda on the table as she pulled her chair closer and leaned over to see what Elise was doing on her computer. "More research?"

Elise nodded slowly. "I can't seem to leave it alone. I keep wondering what in the world I could've missed when Andrea was growing up that's manifesting itself now."

"I see. Well, how about a kiss for now?" Lauren leaned closer.

"I'm so sorry. I didn't mean to ignore you." Elise leaned closer to Lauren as Lauren's arm went around her. Their kiss was sweet but short. "I'm so caught up with Andrea's problem. I can't seem to let it go."

"I understand." Lauren stroked the side of Elise's cheek. "Naturally, you're worried sick about her. Logically, you must know they've got everything under control there at the hospital. They probably even have the Mayo Clinic on speed dial. Thanks to you, Andi has the most state of the art cardiac care around here and outstanding doctors and nurses. She couldn't be in better hands. Emotionally I'm sure you can't help worrying."

Elise rubbed her eyes with the palms of both hands. "My eyeballs feel like they're going to fall out. I guess I need to give it a rest...at least for a while." She sat back in her chair. "So, what've you been up to today?"

"The usual." Lauren sipped from her soda. "That German couple finally decided on a condo and we'll close in a few days. Listen, I'm sure you'll want to be at the hospital again for a while this afternoon, but how about supper? Nothing fancy. I was thinking about a meal for the two of us that doesn't come from the hospital cafeteria."

"I don't know…" Elise's voice trailed off as she gazed out the lanai's sliding doors, seeming to stare at the huge magnolia tree in the back of her yard. "I feel like Andi needs me."

"Sweetie, Andi does need you. I'll bet she could spare you for one evening. I'm thinking that maybe she and Kelly might like to spend an evening together."

Elise looked back at Lauren. "Oh. I guess I hadn't thought of that. I keep feeling like I need to be there with her all the time. I'm only here now because Andrea needed to sleep for a while and the nurse said it'd be best for me to go home. I—"

Lauren interrupted her, taking Elise's hand, and stroking it. "I know, I know. Remember, you aren't all she has now. Kelly's a big part of her life, as well. Why don't you let her take care of Andi?"

Elise took in a deep breath and slowly let it out, looking back at their joined hands. "I'm sure Kelly can take care of her. I guess I…I don't know. I think maybe I'm afraid of losing Andrea. She's all I have left." She swiped at her eye. "My brother's wife, Andrea's mother, died of heart complications after she had Andrea's little brother. They never said what it was, and I'm not sure they knew, since it happened so fast. Then the poor little guy died. I might be flashing back to that. We didn't just lose her mother and my newborn nephew, I lost my brother. He was never the same afterward and immersed himself in his work. That's how I wound up raising Andrea. She's been a real joy in my life. You can understand that this isn't some random fear." This time tears leaked from both eyes, inching their way down her cheeks.

Lauren stroked Elise's cheek, wiping away the tears with her thumb. "Oh, honey, of course it's real. The thought of losing someone you raised, especially someone who thinks of you more as a mom than an aunt, is a terrible thing. I'm sure she feels the same way about the possibility of losing you."

"I hadn't thought about that."

"It's been the two of you for a long time now, from what it sounds like, even when Andi was with her ex. You've been her anchor through all she's had to deal with. Try to remember that she's not all you have. Now there are three of you, four if you count me in, which I hope you do." She gently turned Elise's face up to hers. "I wouldn't want to lose you either."

"I don't have a clue what to do about this situation. I'm feeling something I don't usually feel. Helplessness." Elise's shoulders shook as she began sobbing. "I thought I was okay, but then I keep feeling I should be able to do something other than just sit by her and keep her company. I'm so afraid something's going to happen, and I won't be there with her."

Lauren pulled Elise closer to her. "I know. I know." She held Elise and stroked her back. "I've been through something like what you're going through now. It was some years ago with my former partner. The difference was that I knew she was dying. By the time she was diagnosed, she already had an aggressive, stage four cancer. I almost killed myself trying to be there every second. I didn't want her to die alone in the hospital. Hell, I didn't want her to die at all. Nevertheless, there was no stopping the inevitable. They were able to keep her comfortable and she died peacefully in her sleep."

Elise's face had been buried in Lauren's shoulder. She turned her face up to look at her. "I'm so sorry. I knew you lost a partner. You never mention her, so I didn't think you wanted to talk about her. I honestly don't mind if you want to talk about your ex. It's obvious you loved her, and she was a big part of your life."

Lauren shook her head. "She's gone. I think about her sometimes and I loved her very much, but she's gone. It took me quite a while to get past her loss and move on with my life. You and I are here, now, and I care for you. I didn't see any purpose in bringing up the past or dwelling on sad times."

Elise swiped at her eye with her fingertips. "I'm so glad you're here. I do count you in, as you put it. You're an important part of my life now." She managed a little smile. "All right, you've convinced me. I'll go back to the hospital for a little while this afternoon and then we can enjoy our dinner together and Kelly can be with Andrea this evening without me hanging around."

"Good for you. Look, it's been most of a week now. You'd think if anything awful was going to happen again it would've happened by now. Last time it was...what...just a few days after she got out of the hospital?"

"True. Less than a week after the first time it happened. Now they're waiting for that tear in her artery to heal. She wasn't doing anything strenuous either time, so I don't think they actually know what brought it on."

"I wonder what they'll do when they release her, and they haven't figured it out. Maybe they'll put her on blood thinners and see what happens. That seems to be common after heart attacks."

"Maybe. At least that's what I've seen in some of the stuff online. Sometimes they don't do anything and it simply heals up on its own."

Lauren let out a little sigh. "Well, we can hope that's all she needs. By now you've probably found everything online there is about SCAD, as thorough as you are. On a personal note, and I want you to know I'm not really complaining, we haven't spent a night together since right before she had that second episode. I miss you."

"I miss you too."

Lauren sighed. "But…"

Elise looked away. "I…I just don't know."

"Look, all I want is to hold you while you go to sleep. I want to be here for you. I don't want you to feel alone and worry yourself crazy over Andi by yourself. I want to make sure you understand you're also cared for."

Elise let out a slow sigh. "I know. I'm sorry I haven't had much time for you lately. I feel like I need to concentrate on Andrea and her situation."

"I understand that. But Elise, Kelly has been with her every evening. You've both been there."

"I know…"

"And how is Andi doing now?"

"She seems to be okay."

"Right. So why do you feel like you need to be there all the time?"

"What if something happens? I don't want her to think that I'm not there for her. I'm all the family she has."

"That's the second time you've said that." Lauren sighed.

"I'm sorry, I can't seem to let go of it."

"You're right. You are the only blood relative she has contact with, since her father is out of the picture. However, let's just think this through again. First, you can rest assured that if something happens, she's going to get the best care available. They'll call you and Kelly right away if you're not there. And second, no, you're not the only family she has. You may be the only blood relative in her life, but Kelly is her family now. Believe me, with Kelly around Andi's never going to be alone again. She's very protective. On top of that, I understand Andi's also become quite close to Kelly's friends, Shawn and Carrie."

Another deep sigh. "I guess that's true."

"You know in your heart it is. She still needs you and wants you in her life. No one can ever take your place in her heart. The good thing is that she now has Kelly and some good friends who care about her. I'm not saying you need to spend all the time you're not at the hospital with me. Absolutely not. What I am saying is that you're wearing yourself out. If you don't watch out, you're going to do something that will land you in the hospital like Andi did. Then you won't be much help to her at all, will you?"

"No, I guess deep down I get that. Maybe I'm also concerned because she's my only family left. My brother...well...I told you how he shut me and Andrea out after his wife died. Andrea and I are all that's left. I don't want to lose her."

"Of course you don't. Andi isn't going to die any time soon if Dr. Carter can help it. Didn't she say Andi should heal up completely? Come on. Let's close up that laptop for a while, okay?" Lauren put her hand on the top of the screen and waited. Elise slowly nodded and Lauren closed it and then pushed it toward the middle of the glass-topped table. "I'm sure you need some rest, or at the least to relax a little."

Elise suddenly slammed her hands down on the table, making the whole thing shake. "I hate feeling helpless." She stood up and went to the lanai window facing the pool, her arms wrapped around herself. Lauren followed her. "I take action. I don't just sit and wait for things to happen. I feel like I should be doing something more."

Lauren put her arm around Elise, and then put her other hand on Elise's cheek to turn them face-to-face. "I know, I know. That's the hardest part of this, isn't it? I can't imagine anything else you can do that you haven't already. Now that they figured out what the problem is, you need to trust the doctors and nurses and that hospital you support so considerably. You put the tools in their hands, now you need to trust them to do their job."

Elise crumbled into Lauren's arms, trying to wipe the tears from her eyes before they spilled over. "I'm trying. I'm really trying." She began sobbing uncontrollably and let Lauren hold her while it happened. Her body shook, the tears streaming down her face as she held onto Lauren for dear life.

After a couple of minutes, Lauren steered her over to the sofa and sat her down as she reached for a box of tissues. Then she held Elise close and just let her cry.

CHAPTER NINETEEN

"HI, AUNT ELISE! AND Lauren. What a nice surprise." Andi sat a little more upright on her bed and smoothed out the bedding as Kelly got up to hug both visitors. "Lauren, I don't think you've met our friends Shawn and Carrie."

Lauren reached over to shake hands with Carrie. "Nice to meet you." Then she reached for Shawn's hand. "Hey, you're Kelly's author buddy," she said to Shawn. "I love your books. I'm looking forward to reading the next one."

"Thanks," Shawn said. "Always nice to meet a fan."

Lauren grinned as she watched Elise hugging Andi. "I bet you won't believe this," she said to Andi, "but I talked your aunt into a real meal with me tonight that doesn't include hospital food. She let me tag along on her visit with you."

"Nice. I'm glad you came, Lauren. It's nice to see you again. Aunt Elise, I'm glad you listened to her. That sounds like a great idea."

"Lauren convinced me that you'd be fine under Kelly's watchful eye." Elise looked at Kelly. "I know you won't let me down."

Kelly grinned and looked over at Andi. "Oh, I won't, believe me."

Andi looked at Kelly then around the room at the rest of them. "How did I get so lucky to have such wonderful women in my life?" She reached for Kelly's hand. "If this had happened when I was back in New York with Jo, I might've died. I might never have known what a wonderful life I could've had."

Kelly quickly swiped at her eye with her free hand. "Honey, I believe we were meant to be together. All of us care very much for you. I'm sure you had friends there who would've come to your aid."

"Not like you, Kelly. Or you two, either." She looked at Carrie and Shawn. "I've never had such a wonderful support group before. Aunt Elise and Lauren, you two. My life is so different, so much happier now. I'm not getting all weird, but since you're all here together, I want to tell you how much I value your love and friendship. It means everything to me." She looked around the room at each one of them as she said, "Thank you. I'm truly blessed."

CHAPTER TWENTY

A WEEK AFTER ANDI was released from the hospital, Dr. Carter told her she could do some non-strenuous things like paperwork if she stopped as soon as she felt tired and continued with her cardio rehab. Dr. Carter made her promise, with Kelly as her witness. Andi thought she was going to make her sign a notarized form to that effect, the way she was talking. She knew her doctor was right. She had to get help with her new project. First, she needed to tell Kelly what she had in mind for it.

That evening after dinner as they sat out on the lanai with Piper, she decided it was time. They were snuggling on the loveseat watching the sun go down behind the trees across their back yard. Piper had wormed her way in between them and was enjoying having them both scratch her ears. Andi had rehearsed what she might say, and now the time had come, she felt tongue-tied. Her mind went blank. Then she had a thought.

"Honey, have I told you lately how much I love you?" she asked Kelly.

Kelly laughed a little. "Not in the last hour or so. Feel free to tell me again if you like. I love you too." She gathered Piper into her lap and put her arm around Andi, drawing her closer for a little kiss.

"Mmm...that was nice." She looked up into Kelly's eyes. "You know what, you've inspired me. I watch you making wonderful things out of wood, and I'm sure there are lots of other artists out there who work with wood who could use some exposure. I've made the decision to make this a showcase principally for woodworking items."

"Really?" Kelly answered, eyebrows raised. "That's interesting. I'm surprised there could be enough interest for a whole gallery in wood. Are you sure?"

"I'm sure. I've done my research. Remember I once showed you some pictures of a few items from my SoHo gallery? At the time, you took it all wrong and thought I was trying to court you as an artist, not looking at you as a friend."

Kelly rolled her eyes and shook her head. "I remember that. I'm sorry I misunderstood. You know I don't think of myself as an artist."

"No, you don't. On the other hand, I do think of you that way and I'd bet money Shawn and Carrie do as well. I finally understand that you see yourself making functional things that are also nice to look at. You don't think of them as works of art. After some research, I've discovered quite a few who do woodworking mostly for the art of it. I believe I've found enough of these artists living right here in Florida that I could keep a whole gallery filled with their work. I've been working on this idea for a while, but I didn't want to go any further with it until I talked to you."

Kelly looked at her, head tilted in question. "Why? Is there a problem?"

Andi smiled back at her. "No. No problem. It's just that...well...again back to when we first got to know each other, and you thought I was only interested in you to convince you to make things for my gallery. I want to set the record straight before I go any farther with this, and this is what I want you to know: If you ever decide to make something for display or sale, it will be my pleasure to show it for you. You make beautiful things. However, if you never want to make something for it, that's fine. I never want you to ever feel any pressure again. I do want you to know I would welcome your work."

"Thanks, honey. I appreciate your concern. We seem to be past that hurdle, though. Why are you worried about it now?"

She looked directly into Kelly's eyes. "I love you so much. I don't want anything to ever come between us again. I hadn't told you about it before, well, because I wasn't even sure it was viable. In fact, I originally planned to show mostly Florida-type artwork—you know what I mean, tropical paintings and sculptures and the like. After looking around at what's here, I realized that market is well saturated."

"I can imagine it probably is. There's a big Art Fest here every year, with all kinds of that stuff on display...not to mention the beach galleries and the like."

"Right. That's why I started looking for other ideas and I noticed those pictures I took of our table in the kitchen. You know, the way all those different colored woods flow into each other they look like a painting. That's when it hit me that there must be other people out there making wonderful things out of wood. So, I did some extensive online searches and I've found several woodworking artists right here in Florida."

Kelly's eyes squinted, and she winced as she appeared to consider it. "Hmm…what do they make, sculptures out of cypress knees or the like? I remember seeing stuff like that when I was a kid. To tell you the truth, I wasn't that impressed."

"Well, some of them do, but it's not that kitschy stuff you might've seen at roadside stands years ago. It's amazing what people can make out of driftwood, cypress, palms, or, like you, out of multiple pieces that are put together." She picked up her phone from the side table, tapped and flipped pictures on her phone till she came to a picture of a table. "This was carved out of one piece of wood. Remember this?"

"Oh, yeah. I think I remember that. I asked you why it was in your gallery because it looked like just a cute little table. It was right before you showed me that picture you took of my kitchen table and I got upset with you."

"Right. That artist lives here in Florida, only a couple of hours away. I've convinced him to show here in Fort Myers, as well as in New York. I'm sure he won't get the same kind of exposure here, although you never know who'll walk into a place here in Fort Myers. Tourist season and the Art Fest bring in lots of art lovers."

"Nice! Well, that's a start. I'm glad you told me what you're doing. I'm still sorry I didn't get what you were trying to tell me back then. I guess I jumped to the conclusion that you were just looking for your next 'thing' and I didn't actually listen to what you were saying." Kelly shook her head. "I can be a little hard-headed once in a while."

"No, really?" Andi gave Kelly a playful pat on the cheek. "I think we both can be a bit that way sometimes. You know, I was just as bad when I stayed away from you for months because I was going through my divorce. As it turned out, Jo had already moved on to her next playmate and didn't give a damn what I was doing as long as I signed the divorce papers. She wanted to be free as much as I did. I should've listened to Aunt Elise and told you what was going on. My pigheadedness almost cost me any chance I had with you."

"True. I guess we both messed up in the beginning. All that matters now is that we have each other…and Piper of course." Kelly reached down and scratched Piper's soft little Chihuahua ears, then looked back at Andi. "I love you so much."

"Oh, sweetie, I love you too."

They shared a sweet kiss that began to deepen into something more. Andi could feel her heart quicken and pulled back. "I can't. Not yet."

"But Dr. Carter said you were good to go back to your regular life, as long as you didn't go nuts again and overdo it."

"Yes, that's what she said. You should know, you were there with me."

"Yes, I was. And by regular life, she said we could even make love again, if we weren't planning, as she put it, to do it on horseback, or hanging from the ceiling, or the like. I wasn't planning something like that, although I do miss that part of our lives."

"I know, so do I. Honey, I'm sorry. I'm still scared something's going to happen. I—"

Kelly cut her off. "I understand. Look, I love you and want to make love to you, but I don't want you to be unnecessarily worried. That wouldn't be good. We can wait a while longer, but for now at least we can cuddle. That can't hurt anything."

Andi snuggled closer to Kelly and put her head on Kelly's shoulder. "Cuddling is always good. I want more, but I'd like to be sure of my heart. I'm positive this will eventually get better and I won't be so scared. I feel like I need more time."

"I do understand. Really." Kelly pulled her closer. "I want you to get better and will do everything I can to help you."

"What you're doing right now is helping more than you know."

CHAPTER TWENTY-ONE

"MICHAEL, I NEED TO talk to you about something." Andi moved the phone to her other ear. "I've decided I need some help down here, and I'd like you to come down and help me get this new place up and running."

"Really? Are you sure?" The voice on the other end sounded doubtful. "I thought you wanted this new one to be all your own baby. That's why I haven't offered any assistance before now."

Andi took a deep breath and let it out as she paced the room slowly as part of her cardiac exercise program. "I'm sure. I should've asked for help a while ago. I did want this one to be mine from the beginning, and it will be. Right now, I'm under doctor's orders to sit back a bit and start getting more sleep."

She heard Michael's voice soften. "We're all sorry to hear you've been sick."

She smiled. "Thanks. I'm getting better every day. Look, you've been doing a great job with the store up there. I'm sorry I've had to put all of that on you for a few weeks now. If you don't feel like you can leave there for a bit, just say so. Maybe Serena could come down for a while. Either way, I'll pay for your housing while you're here, along with a rental car. I'm sure we can find you a furnished condo in town for the duration. What do you think?"

"Hey, a free vacation in Florida. Not bad." She could imagine the grin on his face.

"I'm not renting you a condo at the beach, Michael." Andi laughed. "And it's not going to be much of a vacation most of the time. I'm sure you'll manage to make some time to see the sights and work on a tan."

"Tell you what, let me talk this over with my other half. Do you have any idea how long this will take? I mean, are we talking a few weeks...a month or maybe two?"

Andi took a drink from her water bottle. "I'm thinking about six weeks, two months outside. I'm willing to fly your honey down here for conjugal visits. We don't want you to be unhappy here."

Michael chuckled. "Well, since you're putting it that way...for now, assume I'm coming, but don't rent the condo until I get back to you. I should be able to have that conversation this evening and call you back tomorrow. How's that?"

"Fair enough. I need whoever's coming to be down here by early next week, if at all possible. If you can't come, please talk to Serena about this, since you're her boss. I'll offer her the same terms as I'm offering you, including flying her husband and kids down. When you call me back tomorrow, I need to know who's coming, if either of you can. And Michael?"

"Yes?"

"Thank you from the bottom of my heart for the good work you do up there. While you're here, if you're the one who comes, you'll need to fly back to New York to take care of anything major up there. Meantime, email and the like will need to suffice, like they did for me. I can't imagine how that place would stay open without you, with me down here so much."

"You're welcome. I love my job. I love this gallery. And, of course, we love you up here. Look, we're so glad you're finally happy. You are, right?"

Andi smiled. "Oh, yeah, I'm very happy. I've found my life here with Kelly. That doesn't mean I don't care about you guys, but I've finally found where I belong. Does that make sense?"

"It makes all the sense in the world. I know you inherited me when you bought the SoHo gallery and I'm glad you kept me around. Making me second in command meant a lot to me; it meant you trusted me...a lot more than the previous owner did. He micromanaged everything. You let me make some decisions and let me flounder occasionally. I appreciate that and learned a lot from it. I hope to always do well for you."

"I know you will. Anyway, please call me tomorrow with what the deal is, who's coming, and all that as early in the day as possible."

"I will. Now about that Sanders exhibit..."

***

A short while later, Andi finally hit end on the call, plopped down on the sofa, and dropped her phone on the coffee table. She heaved a sigh and leaned back into the cushions. She couldn't believe how tired she felt, although she hadn't been on the phone that long. She had been walking like the rehab doctor told her to, and it was tiring. It was a good thing she'd given in and asked Michael for help.

Michael Stewart was a good man who knew a lot about artwork as well as the business end of running an art gallery. If he could be the one that came to assist her, she knew she could relax a bit more and still get the place opened soon.

His always calm demeanor was one of his biggest assets. That and whenever he said he would take care of something, he did. She didn't need to check up on him. She didn't need to ask him twice. She didn't have to wonder if it was okay. It was done and done right. The few times she had allowed him to make a decision that didn't work out like he planned were learning experiences he needed to have. Now in his fifties, he was quite ready to run the place all by himself, and he had been, for the most part, since she decided to live in Florida. Someday, he'd probably leave her to open his own art gallery. She seriously hoped it wasn't going to be any time soon.

She decided to lie down on the sofa for a little while. Since she wasn't allowed to go back to a full workday yet—and she knew in her heart that was the right thing to do—she had taken to afternoon naps after her morning cardio rehab. They helped her feel better during the evenings and recuperate from the mornings. Andi found herself hoping this wasn't going to be how the rest of her life went—rehab and naps. And no sex. Dr. Carter said they could return to lovemaking, but she just wasn't ready. She thought again that she was way too young for that kind of life. Maybe when she was in her eighties... She smiled to herself as she closed her eyes. Yeah, right. Make that nineties.

Maybe if she could get through the grand opening without any new health issues, then she'd feel safe. Maybe.

CHAPTER TWENTY-TWO

"YOU'LL LIKE MICHAEL," ANDI told Kelly as they drove to the airport. "I know he has the company credit card to rent his car and all that, so we didn't really have to come. I'm pretty sure he's never been to Fort Myers before, so I thought it'd be nice to meet him there."

Kelly pulled their clasped hands to her lips for a kiss. "I'm sure I'll like him. Is he coming alone? I forgot to ask if he's bringing his husband with him."

Andi smiled. "David? He's coming next weekend for a few days. He had a project to finish before he took some time off. Did I tell you he's an attorney?"

"I don't recall hearing what he did. An attorney, huh? Well, I'm sure he'll be interesting to talk with."

"I know you're being funny, but he actually is an interesting person. I'm looking forward to having you meet them both."

"I'm so relieved you decided to get some help setting up your new place. I feel much better now that Michael's coming."

"So do I. He's looking forward to working on this with me, and I'm sure we can get it up and running much quicker than I could've by myself. Besides, he's fun to have around. I think I've missed having someone else to work with down here."

"Hey! What about me?" Kelly asked.

"Oh, sweetie, you're wonderful. To tell you the truth, to be able to talk about things you're excited about with someone who gets a high off the same things, that's especially nice."

"I care about your work. I honestly do."

Andi nodded slowly. "Yes, I know you do. Here's a for instance: I have no idea what most of your tools are or how they're used. Anything other than a hammer or a screwdriver is completely lost on me. Don't you enjoy a nice conversation sometimes with someone else who's as passionate about the same things you are? Someone you don't have to explain things to? Comparing notes, for instance, on projects or new tools, it's obvious you're enjoying yourself. That time you and Carrie's boss got into a long conversation at their office luncheon, your face just lit up. That's kind of how it is for me."

"When you put it that way..."

"It makes sense. I'm looking forward to having Michael here to work with every day for a while. I'd almost forgotten how much I loved talking shop with him." She grinned. "I can see that you're beginning to understand now."

"I do." Kelly squeezed Andi's hand. "Your eyes get almost a twinkle in them when you're talking about it. I wish I could help you more than I have so far."

"If there's anything you can help with, believe me I'll ask you immediately. I'd never hire a carpenter for something there without talking to you first."

Kelly chuckled. "That's good to know. I wouldn't want you to pay someone else for something I can do for you."

Andi waggled her eyebrows and grinned. "Oh, honey, there are obviously some things I would never want anyone else to do but you." She laughed and leaned back in her seat.

Kelly felt the blood rush to her cheeks and managed a laugh. "It's hard to believe you can still do that to me. I thought you'd gotten tired of making me blush." She reached one hand up to rub her cheek as she turned onto Terminal Access Road, leading into the airport.

Andi grinned and stroked Kelly's arm. "Never, sweetie. You're too cute when you're a bit embarrassed." A minute later, the grin was replaced by a more serious look. "I'm sorry, I guess I shouldn't be teasing you like that right now, but I can't help it."

"Oh, that's all right. It makes things feel more like normal, doesn't it?"

"Yes, it does. I'm sure we'll get completely back to normal soon." She reached for Kelly's hand and squeezed it. "By the way, Michael's being a little mysterious about something."

"Hmm...do you have any inkling what that's about?"

"Nope. He simply said he had something he wanted to talk to me about when he gets here. When I pressed him for details, he insisted it was something he wanted to talk to me about in person."

"That does sound mysterious. No clue what it could be, huh?"

"None. It wasn't connected to anything we were talking about, like a 'by the way' while we were talking about something else. He just said there was something that he'd like to discuss with me. I sure hope he isn't thinking about leaving."

Kelly glanced over at Andi, then back at the road. "He wouldn't move away if his husband works in New York, right?"

"No, I can't see them moving away. He might've gotten an offer from another gallery though. He's very good at what he does."

"Well, I'm sure he'll tell you in due time. Since we'll be together for supper tonight, maybe he'll bring it up then. That is, unless he wants to talk to you alone. If it's business, he might wait till tomorrow while you're at the shop."

"I guess. I've already decided not to worry about it, whatever it is. I'm more curious than anything else right now. One thing I think I've learned from my heart attack is that some things aren't worth stressing over, and this is one of them." She shrugged. "I'll have to wait to see what he wants to talk to me about and not try to guess."

"Wow! Look at you. Now, that's a very healthy attitude. You have learned something from all of this. I'm proud of you."

"I'm proud of me too. Now, if I could just learn to cook..." Andi laughed.

CHAPTER TWENTY-THREE

"ALL RIGHT, MICHAEL, HERE'S what I have in mind for this space." Andi unrolled a large sheet of drawing paper. "As I mentioned at dinner Sunday night, this will be, at least for now, mostly woodworking sculptural pieces. There might be some wall art, as well. We'll want to showcase these things so each one gets enough attention."

Michael put his hand on the paper to hold one end down, then the other one on Andi's shoulder. "You know, we can do this sitting down. Let's do this the easy way for now, okay?"

She looked him in the eyes. "I'm not—"

"No, you're not an invalid. No, you don't need to be treated like you're going to break. I'm just saying we should use your energy wisely." He pulled a couple of folding chairs over to the worktable and pointed. "Sit."

She sat. So did he.

"All right then." He smiled at her. "Now let's get this show on the road." He turned back to look at the drawings on the table.

She put her hand on his arm. "Still not going to tell me what you wanted to talk to me about?"

He turned to her and smiled. "Not yet. Let's deal with this first. Don't worry, I'm not going anywhere, if that's what you're worried about."

"Thanks for clearing that up. The first thing I thought of was that you'd gotten a job offer from someone else."

"Oh, I get those off and on. But to tell you the truth, money isn't everything and I happen to like where I am, thank you very much." He grinned. "Besides, David's office is close enough for us to meet for lunch or dinner. We sometimes eat breakfast near there before work. We like that."

"I wasn't aware that David's office was that close. I thought his firm was on Park Avenue. Did they move their office, or did he move to another law practice?"

Michael smiled. "He resigned his old position and opened up his own office."

"Wow. Good for him. When did that happen?"

"Oh, about six months ago."

"Really? That long ago? I'm sorry I've been so preoccupied that I haven't kept up on what's important with my friends. I honestly can't believe I didn't know. I thought he was happy where he was."

"It was okay." Michael shrugged. "He was making very good money and he even made partner early in his career. However, he's now in a position to help our community more. He said several times while he was with his old firm that it was time to give back and he decided to make it work. He and a couple of guys and a woman he's known since college decided to open a firm dedicated to the legal needs of the LGBT community. Of course, they don't discriminate, and they take on other clients sometimes. Their practice though, targets people like us."

Andi nodded. "Now that's really nice. I'm sure you're very proud of him."

A grin lit up Michael's face. "Oh, I am, believe me. He's an excellent attorney and I've been impressed with his new legal partners as well. Their new firm is doing very well. Anyway, we can talk later about what you and I need to talk about." He put his finger on the plans. "Let's get this up and running first, then we can have our discussion."

"All right, Michael. Right now let me tell you one more time how grateful I am that you're here."

Michael put his arms around Andi for a hug. "Boss Lady, I'm glad to be here and happy you wanted my help. This will be a great experience for both of us." He released her. "You make the decisions and let me do the legwork for you, at least to start. You need to save your energy for the craziness to come when it gets closer to opening. Is that a deal?"

Andi held out her hand, which Michael gripped in a firm handshake. "Deal," she said.

CHAPTER TWENTY-FOUR

"I HAVE AN ANNOUNCEMENT to make," Andi said. She, Kelly, Michael, and David had gathered out on the lanai at Kelly and Andi's house with drinks after a pizza delivery dinner. "I've come up with a name for my new place, and Michael agrees it will work. Now I'd like to hear how you rate it, as completely unbiased members of the public."

"Completely unbiased, of course," Kelly said as a grin lit up her face. "Let's hear it."

"I'm ready," David said.

Andi bit on her lower lip for a second, then grinned. "Okay, what do you two think of the name Heartwood Gallery? How does that sound to you?"

"Heartwood Gallery. I like it. There are lots of things you can do, logo-wise, with a name like that," Kelly said.

"I like it, Andi. It has a nice sound to it." David held up his glass of wine. "Here's to Heartwood. All the success in the world."

The others held up their glasses, clinked them together in a toast, then they all took a celebratory sip from their drinks.

"Thanks." Andi took another sip from her glass. "I'm glad you all like it, because I ordered a sign today." She laughed. "I was sure you'd like it as much as I do, since it kind of says what it is. Wooden items made from the heart. Every artist works hard on each piece, bringing it to life. I wanted to express that in the name of this place."

"It's very fitting," Michael said. "We have several artists lined up already and should be able to make the grand opening announcement as soon as the sign is up and then open in a few weeks. I'm already working on a guest list and invitations, which Andi here will have the final approval on."

Andi smiled. "I'm so glad you're here, Michael. I wanted to do this by myself, but I'm finding that although I'm still making the decisions, having your help has made all the difference in the world. Just another person to make phone calls and help me talk to artists has helped so much. You've taken a lot off my shoulders."

Michael grinned. "I'm loving this. It's so much fun being in on the ground floor of something new. I can't thank you enough for letting me have this experience."

"You're thanking me?" Andi laughed. "I'm the one who needed the help. I appreciate you coming down here and David for being so understanding. I know it's asking a lot of both of you. It's hard to be apart."

David put his hand on Michael's, looked into Michael's eyes, and then over at Andi. "I wouldn't want him to miss out on this opportunity to do something new. I'm behind him all the way. I'm behind both of you. I'm sure it's going to be wonderful."

Andi nodded. "Thank you. We're doing our best and we'll find out soon enough. The biggest pieces will be arriving in about ten days. We'll have time to get them situated and we'll work the rest of the items around them afterward without making the display look claustrophobic."

Kelly looked over at David, who was obviously enjoying watching his husband in his element. Andi and Michael almost glowed with happiness doing what they loved. "So, David, these two seem to be having a great deal of fun with this. It doesn't seem like that much work to me." She grinned as Andi's and Michael's mouths fell open. "I'm kidding, of course. I know how much planning has gone into this project, with the long hours and research." She put her arm around Andi. "I'm sure it'll turn out great and you'll both have something to be proud of."

Andi snuggled into Kelly's side. "Thanks, honey. This project would be much, much harder without the love and support you and David have given us. I hope you both get that."

"I agree. This is Andi's baby, but I'm having a great time helping deliver it," Michael said.

Andi patted Kelly on the leg and smiled up at her. "By the way, we're going to need some help with the display space soon, if you're interested and have time. I should have the dimensions of the items arriving in a couple of days and could use some platforms to display them on. Could you make us some nice pedestals and a few shelves?"

"I'd love to. I was just waiting for you to ask."

"Great," Andi said. "And David, I've a favor to ask of you also, if you don't mind."

"Shoot. I'm at your disposal."

"Michael says you have outstanding taste in beverages. We'd love it if you could advise us on something nice to serve. I'd like the usual champagne and wine, but something a bit less ostentatious, along with some non-alcoholic selections. I want our artists and other guests to feel comfortable."

"I'd be happy to. When you're ready, you can give me your budget, how many guests you're expecting, and I can handle that."

Andi put her hand up. "Wait a minute. I didn't mean that you had to actually order it or anything."

"Oh, no, it's okay. I have a guy. He knows where to get almost anything anywhere for a great price. Believe me, I'd love to do this for you."

Michael grinned at his husband before looking back at Andi. "I forgot to tell you that in another life he'd be an unbelievably wonderful party planner. He loves this stuff."

Andi grinned back at David as she nodded. "Well, okay then. You've got to be busy with clients."

"We have an amazing staff working with us. Besides, all it'll take is a phone call and it'll be taken care of. I can do it from my desk at work when you let me know what you need. It'll be fun." David put his arm around Michael. "Besides, now I won't feel left out."

"I do appreciate it. And we wouldn't want anyone to feel left out now, would we?" Andi laughed.

CHAPTER TWENTY-FIVE

THE NEXT FEW WEEKS were taken up focusing on Andi's new venture. The walls were redone, Kelly built new pedestals for incoming artwork, and Michael and Andi began installing the incoming pieces with the artists. It wasn't long till Heartwood Gallery was looking exactly like it was supposed to. Passers-by were starting to look in the windows once the sign was up.

Andi spent one afternoon interviewing web services. She could've used the one she had in New York, but she was trying to use a local company just to make this venture entirely a Florida business. By the end of the day, she found what she wanted, a local woman who was involved with the Art Festival. They hit it off immediately, and in no time at all, Andi knew she had found another friend there in Fort Myers, as well as an outstanding webmaster.

It was all coming together. All the licenses and odds and ends were falling into place as if they were always meant to be. She found some great office furniture through one of the artists she was showcasing. She even found a couple of part-time employees through a local art school.

And Michael was here, there, everywhere, helping to make things happen. He worked in the New York trips to the SoHo location seamlessly, as if he had always been juggling things. Plus, those short trips gave him a night at home with David. She was so happy she'd decided to let Michael help her. As David had said, it was a great opportunity for him and a great help for her. All in all, a win-win situation.

In the back of her head, though, Andi knew something was coming. Michael had an important matter to talk to her about that was apparently momentous enough that he was going to wait till after the opening to tell her about it. She tried to pry it out of him a few more times, but every time she tried, he simply laughed it off and told her it would wait.

She was also a bit worried about Aunt Elise, who had gone back to

New York for a couple of weeks—for work, she said. It was unlike her not to call for a couple of days. When Andi did talk to her, she seemed fine. Apparently, Aunt Elise hadn't been calling Lauren any more often than that, which was odd as well. She hoped they were okay.

Andi was sure, from what she'd seen, that Lauren was perfect for her aunt and Elise was completely taken with Lauren. For Aunt Elise to run up to New York and be gone for a couple of weeks during her time in Florida was unheard-of, unless there was an emergency. She would've mentioned something like that. She'd only said that she'd be back in time for the grand opening. She had promised, and Aunt Elise always kept her promises. Always.

Finally, the opening was a day away and everything seemed perfect. She had a backup plan for everything she could think of that could go wrong. Even the weather was supposed to cooperate. She anticipated a great turnout according to the RSVP responses she'd received from some local dignitaries who were her aunt's friends, insuring the event would be featured in the local media. There was one artist who was bringing a few small items with her the morning of the show opening, but other than that, everything was ready.

She sat at her desk, thumbing through the featured items catalog that would be handed out at the opening and shown on the Heartwood website. The only pieces that didn't make it into the catalog were those few small items coming in tomorrow. Michael had made a last-minute run to New York. He and David were flying in this evening, ready to enjoy the fruits of their time apart and taking a few days after the opening for a well-deserved vacation together at Fort Myers Beach.

A knock on her open office door roused her from her thoughts. When she looked up, there stood Kelly, grinning from ear to ear. Andi couldn't help smiling back. "All right, what's got you all happy faced?" she said as she closed the catalog.

Kelly leaned casually against the door frame, her arms folded. "Oh, just here to pick up my favorite girl. I thought maybe you'd like to enjoy a nice, quiet dinner downtown, since there are lots of great eateries within walking distance. What do you think?"

Andi tossed the catalog onto a pile of them and stood up, took the few steps to her lover, and put her arms around her, leaning into Kelly's embrace. "I think I'm happier than anyone has a right to be. Everything seems to be working out. I'd be lying if I said I wasn't anticipating something happening. You know, if things seem too perfect, they usually are. Right this minute I'd love to take a walk and have dinner with you."

Kelly held her out at arm's length, gazing into her eyes. "I'm so proud of you. You've done a wonderful job on this place. If anything goes wrong tomorrow, I'm confident we can handle it. Agreed?"

"Absolutely." Andi's phone went off, Elise's familiar ringtone. Andi pulled the phone from her pocket. "Aunt Elise! Are you back?"

Andi heard a sigh on the other end. "No, I'm not. But I'll be back for your opening, I swear. There was more to do here than I had anticipated. It's looking like I'll be on an early afternoon flight out of here tomorrow. I'll still arrive in time to change and get to Heartwood in time for the opening. I promised you, and I've always done everything in my power to keep my promises, haven't I?"

"Yes, you have. You always have. Are you all right? You never did say what it was that you had to go back for."

"Oh, you know, stuff at the publishing house and some other things I needed to be here in person for. No matter. I'll see you at your preview opening tomorrow evening. And sweetheart..."

"Yes?"

"I'm so proud of you and happy for you. I wanted to make sure to tell you that I couldn't be happier about your new gallery and that you're finally with someone who truly loves you and supports what you want to do. I don't have to worry about you anymore."

"Oh, good. Now I can take up bungee jumping and skydiving." Andi smothered a laugh.

She could hear Elise's laugh on the other end. "Don't even think of it! You don't want to give me a stroke, now do you? All right, young lady. No more even joking about that. Let me catch my breath for a bit first. Anyway, I'll see you and Kelly tomorrow. I love you both very much."

"You know we love you right back. I hope everything goes okay up there and you have a safe trip home." Andi hit end on the call and looked at Kelly as she shook her head slowly. "Aunt Elise sounded funny. She said she's not coming in till tomorrow afternoon in time to be here for the opening. I wonder if Lauren has a clue as to what's going on."

"Knowing Elise, she's probably fine. Let's try to remember to call Lauren after dinner and find out what she knows," Kelly said. "For now, let's just enjoy ourselves. Tomorrow's going to be very hectic with the opening and all, so I thought we could spend this evening together relaxing. Kind of like the calm before the storm."

Andi melted into Kelly's arms, her head on her shoulder. She took a deep breath and let it out slowly. "It's going to happen, isn't it? All the work that went into this place, and tomorrow it's going to open. I still find it hard to believe."

"Believe it. You're the one that made it happen. You had some help, but this baby is all yours."

Andi laughed. "Does that mean you're not going to help with diaper changes and midnight feedings?"

"Don't even go there," Kelly said, emphasizing the word 'even' as she put up her hand. "I'll support you in any way I can, but it's all yours. All. Yours."

CHAPTER TWENTY-SIX

THE EVENING HEARTWOOD GALLERY held its private opening was lovely. The location was only a block from the mile-wide Caloosahatchee River, and the light breeze from the water made its way up the street, barely ruffling Kelly's hair as she stood outside the door. She ran her fingers through her hair once more and tugged a little at the jacket she rarely wore, but was happy to sport on this occasion for Andi.

This preview event was invitation-only, with the public grand opening and ribbon-cutting tomorrow morning, and although it was a dressy occasion, it didn't require evening gowns or tuxes. The invitations specified the dress code as sport coats and dinner dresses.

Andi had bought a new dress for this evening's event. When Andi had come downstairs all dressed, Kelly was sure her eyes would bug out of her head. She was beautiful, with her blonde hair pulled up simply into a pretty clip. She had turned around slowly for Kelly to admire her lovely cobalt Zac Posen dress. From the wide scoop neckline and cap sleeves down to the fitted bodice and flared skirt, it looked just like something Audrey Hepburn would have worn years ago. And it suited her perfectly. It was exactly what she needed to give her confidence for the evening. Kelly knew she'd have a hard time looking at anyone but Andi all evening.

Kelly hadn't seen Lauren or Elise yet, although the opening wasn't for another half hour. When they had talked to Lauren last night, she was as much in the dark about what Elise was up to in New York. She hadn't heard any more than they had, and Elise had been just as noncommittal to her as she had to Andi when questioned. She had told Lauren the same thing—'that she'd be there tonight.'

Andi and Michael were busy inside with the artists, and to Andi's delight, David had happily taken over dealing with the caterer. Kelly was starting to feel a little bit useless, although she knew that wasn't so. She'd built all the display areas to Andi's specifications and that was as important to presenting all the pieces. Within a few minutes, Kelly saw Shawn and Carrie walking up the street and she felt her whole body relax a bit. They were exactly what she needed.

Carrie gave her a hug. "So, what are you, the guard keeping out the riffraff?"

"Nope, that's Jeffrey's job over there." She pointed to the young man at the door holding a clipboard. "He's one of the art students Andi hired to help out at the store. I just came out here for some fresh air and to watch for another familiar face or two."

Shawn hugged her, and then patted her on the back. "From what I can see through the window, here, it looks very nice. I'm looking forward to seeing what she came up with. Showing only Florida woodworking artisans is an intriguing idea. Definitely different."

"Tell you the truth, I'm very pleasantly surprised. I kidded her early on about having a bunch of carved cypress knees and the like. It turns out Florida has a lot of very talented artists who happen to work in wood. I think you'll be surprised as much as I was."

Carrie smiled. "I'm looking forward to it. By the way, are Elise and Lauren here yet? I didn't see either of their cars parked nearby."

"Nope. No, wait...here comes Lauren." Kelly waved at Lauren as she strode down the sidewalk looking dashing in a plum shirt, a dressy pair of black slacks, and a black jacket. "Look at you," she said to Lauren. "You clean up very nicely."

"Actually, this is more like work attire. At least for some of my clients." Lauren laughed and put her arm around Kelly. "I can work with you in shorts if I want to."

"True." Kelly looked around. "Have you talked to Elise? I figured she'd be with you."

Lauren pressed her lips together, eyebrows raised. "She called me yesterday and said to come on by myself. She was going to be short on time and she'd drive her own car. Obviously, she's not here yet, so that's sure cutting it close. I know Andi is counting on her to be here at the start."

"Well, she promised she'd be here. And guess what, here she comes." Kelly looked at her watch. "With five minutes to spare."

Kelly caught Carrie staring at Elise as she walked across the street. "What's the matter?"

"You don't think she looks different?" Carrie whispered to them.

"Come to think of it, she does," Lauren whispered back and appeared to think for a second. "I can't put my finger on what's different, but something is."

They watched and waved as Elise walked toward them. Her smile lit up her face as she saw them waving. The simple black sheath-style dress did her justice, as did those Jimmy Choo pumps in which Elise walked so confidently.

Kelly looked over at Lauren and whispered, "Better scrape your chin off the ground. You're definitely staring." When Lauren looked over at her, she grinned. "If you were a cartoon, your eyeballs would be on springs, jumping out of their sockets." They both shook their heads and laughed.

Carrie was first to reach Elise, hugging her as she complimented her on her dress and telling her how nice she looked. Shawn reached to shake hands, instead, Elise reached to give her a hug.

Kelly was next to give Elise a hug. "Right on time, as you promised. I know someone inside who's anxiously waiting for you to arrive."

Lauren reached for Elise's hand. "This someone has been looking for you, as well." As Lauren gave her a hug, Kelly heard Lauren telling Elise, "You look amazing." Elise smiled back and murmured a simple, "Thank you. Would you walk me in?"

"I'd be honored," Lauren said, offering Elise her arm.

The rest of the evening went off without a hitch. Several of the major pieces were sold, to be delivered after the initial show was over. The local press took lots of pictures with Andi, Elise, and various artists and dignitaries in attendance.

Elise was busy going from guest to guest with Andi introducing her to the ones she didn't already know, making small talk, and discussing the various pieces of artwork. Lauren was impressed that Elise had done her homework and knew something about every artist, nearly as much as Andi did. She realized she shouldn't have been surprised that Elise had brushed up before the show. That was pure Elise. It's what she was good at, making people comfortable and playing the perfect hostess.

Lauren also knew quite a few of the guests and was happy to tell them that she had found the gallery space for Andi, when asked. She also made a point of mentioning that Kelly had done the interior work on the store, pointing her out and introducing her to a few people. But Lauren spent most of the evening watching Elise and trying not to obviously stare.

She still couldn't put her finger on what it was that was different about Elise. It was as if she was seeing her for the first time. Maybe their time apart had done this. Whatever it was she was totally entranced. Every so often, Elise looked her way and smiled. Oh, that smile. It could easily melt her from the inside out. Sometimes Elise would beckon her over to meet someone she thought Lauren should be acquainted with, introduce them, and then move on to talk with another guest.

All Lauren knew was that she couldn't take her eyes off her. Elise could've asked her to go jump off the building that evening and she probably would've done it without hesitation. This wasn't like her at all to be all bug-eyed over anyone. Tonight she couldn't help it.

As the evening wound down and most of the guests had gone, Lauren saw Andi disappear into her office with her assistant, Michael. She assumed they were talking about how the opening went, business-wise. Michael's husband was making sure the catering crew finished cleaning up, and Kelly was busy talking with a couple near the door. Lauren looked around and realized Elise was nowhere to be seen.

When Kelly closed the door behind the last guests, Lauren asked her, "Have you seen Elise? I could have sworn she was just here, but she seems to have disappeared."

"She left a couple of minutes ago. Shawn and Carrie were walking her to her car. She said she was going to say goodnight to you before she left. I guess she didn't?"

"That was probably the one time I went to the restroom. Maybe she thought I left already. Well, at least she's safe getting to her car in the dark."

Kelly looked pointedly at her. "Something wrong between you two? I mean, I can see you're still quite taken with her, but..."

Lauren shrugged. "I thought we were great. Then I only talked to her a couple of times while she was gone on this sudden mysterious trip of hers...her choice. When she came back, she didn't want me to pick her up this evening. I have no idea what's going on. The looks she gave me tonight were nice, even though we hardly spent any time together. I assumed she was in hostess mode, helping Andi out. Still, it feels very odd."

Kelly patted Lauren on her shoulder. "True. If it's any consolation, Elise didn't call Andi much either, while she was gone. I hope you can figure it out soon and everything will be all right."

"Me too. Maybe she's trying to work something out. I don't know if this is her way of backing away from our relationship, or if she wants or needs some space. I guess she'll tell me when she's ready."

"Well, you know Elise. She's not going to be mean about it no matter what's going on. I'm sure she'll explain it soon. It looks like you'll just have to be patient and hang on."

Lauren gave a wan smile. "I'm trying to be patient. I really have been. It's hard."

Before Kelly could say anything else, Andi and Michael came out of the office, both chatting and smiling. Andi walked over to Kelly, putting her arm around her waist. "Thanks, honey, for all you did to make this happen. And Lauren, you had a lot to do with this, too, since you helped me find the perfect spot."

"You're welcome," Lauren said. "Congratulations. It appears this evening was quite a success. I saw sold tags on several very nice items and that should look great tomorrow for the ribbon cutting and public opening."

Andi beamed. "Yes, it will. Very nice. Giving credit where credit is due, I have to say Aunt Elise had a lot to do with it. She's quite the saleslady." She laughed. "Maybe I should hire her to work for me."

Kelly laughed. "I heard her telling one gentleman how nice a particular piece would look in a specific spot in his law office, and he wound up buying it. Obviously, he had to be someone she knew quite well. Then again, Elise seemed to be familiar with most of the guests, didn't she?"

Andi nodded. "She should. She's the one who gave us most of the invitation list for tonight's preview. I added a few more people, but to tell you the truth, this was pretty much her party, guest-wise. I told her several times how much I appreciated everything she did for me this evening. I didn't see her leave, so I must've been talking to Michael when she went home."

"Shawn and Carrie walked her out to her car," Kelly said. "When she said good night, she looked a bit tired. It's been a long day for her, I bet."

"I'm sure," Lauren said. "I think I'd better get going." She reached to shake Andi's hand. "It's been a real pleasure working with you on this venture. It looks like it's going to be a great success and if you decide to branch out to a second Florida location, say in Naples or Sarasota, I'd be happy to help you out. Meantime, I hope to see you again soon."

Andi looked at Lauren, still holding onto her hand with both of hers, "I'm sure we'll be seeing you around often. Aunt Elise is quite fond of you, you know."

"Well, I thought so. We'll see. I'm very fond of her also. Goodnight everyone."

Before Andi and Kelly could say anything else, Lauren had turned for the door and Michael and David came over. "So, did you tell Kelly what we talked about yet?" Michael asked.

"Not yet. I haven't had a chance." Andi turned to Kelly. "Michael and David want to buy me out of the SoHo gallery."

Kelly's mouth dropped open as she looked back and forth from Andi to Michael. "Really? I mean, wow. That is quite a surprise. This is what Michael wanted to talk to you about?"

Andi laughed and looked back at Michael and David. "Yeah, and I have to admit I was caught completely off guard."

Michael looked over at David, and then back at Andi and Kelly. "David and I've been talking about it for a while and it's a sincere offer. We thought maybe it'd be less stressful for Andi to only have one gallery to run, right here in town. Plus, I believe I'm ready to run the SoHo place on my own now, if she's ready to let it go."

Andi nodded. "I told Michael that I need to think about it. It was my first venture and I have a lot of myself invested in it. I'm not sure if I can let it go yet. I told him I'd give them an answer in a week or two, giving me time to let things settle down a bit here so I can make a clear-headed decision."

David put his arm around Michael. "We're in no rush. We think the SoHo location would be a great investment, and I have faith in Michael's ability to manage it. We'll let you lock up now. I took care of the caterer and everything is ready to close. Think about what we offered and let us know one way or the other when you're ready."

Andi gave each man a hug. "David, thank you so much for your help with the opening. I can't begin to tell you how much I appreciate the sacrifice you made, having Michael here for so long, and on top of that, handling the caterer and beverages. If you ever decide to get out of the law business, you'd make a great event planner. And Michael, you're amazing. Your help means everything to me. Merely having you here has made a big difference, let alone all the work you put in."

Michael grinned. "Our pleasure. All that's left for me now is to help you get the public opening off to a good start tomorrow and then we're off for our little vacation at the beach. My toes are ready for some sand."

CHAPTER TWENTY-SEVEN

IT WAS LATE WHEN Andi and Kelly finally got home. They were barely inside when Piper came running to greet them. She insisted on being picked up to place puppy kisses on both their faces. Within a couple of minutes, Piper was finished with her greeting and was ready to get down and get a treat. Once Piper was settled with one of her cookies, Andi smiled and turned to Kelly as she put her arms around her, drawing her very close for a kiss.

"Thank you for all you've done to help make tonight happen. I love you so much." She kissed her again.

"Mmm...nice," Kelly whispered into Andi's ear. "I love you, honey." She backed away, as she usually did of late. "You look amazing tonight." She twirled Andi around. "I'm sure you want to get that dress off now. Would you like anything before we go to bed? I think there's some rocky road ice cream in the freezer. I could bring you some."

Andi shook her head. "As much as I love rocky road, I'll pass. I'm ready for bed now. How about you?"

"Sounds good to me."

A few minutes later, Kelly was lying in bed, waiting for Andi to join her. She played in her head the many times they'd made love in that bed, and the many nights they had not since Andi became so involved with her new endeavor, and especially since her two heart attacks. The fear Andi had of having another attack kept her from getting closer to Kelly than a cuddle, but at least they'd had that. Kelly longed to make love to her, to feel her, to hear her. It had been so long. Cuddles were better than nothing.

Shortly, she felt Andi slide into bed in the darkened room. Kelly put out her arm to pull Andi into their usual snuggle. Andi's lips were on hers as their bodies touched. Although they had continued to sleep in the nude, this was not the same kind of touch. Andi draped her body over Kelly's as she kissed her, her hands touching Kelly in areas that hadn't been touched for some time. Kelly's pulse quickened as she wrapped her arms around the woman she loved, and their kisses deepened.

Andi pulled back and put her hand on Kelly's cheek. "I love you so much, honey. I hope you know that."

"I know you do," Kelly said. "I love you too. Are you sure you're ready for this? Please don't do something you're not ready for. I don't—"

Andi interrupted Kelly with a finger to her lips, and then another kiss. "I know what I'm doing. I want this. I've missed making love with you and I want you right now."

Kelly pulled her closer. "Sweetie, I want you more than you can imagine. I never stopped wanting you."

"Show me." Andi softly kissed Kelly's lips. "Please? I want it to be like it was."

Without another word, Kelly's hands and mouth made love to the woman she adored. She took her sweet time, touching and kissing everywhere on Andi she had missed for months. Their kisses warmed her to her core. She nearly cried when she heard Andi cry out her release, her own coming shortly after. They held each other tightly afterward, relief washing over them as they knew they were going to be all right.

Kelly brushed Andi's hair back with her fingers, gazing into her eyes like she'd never seen those lovely eyes before. "I love you more than I can tell you," she whispered. "I hope you feel my love every day forever."

Andi tenderly kissed Kelly's lips. "I love you and hope nothing ever keeps us apart again. I'll always love you."

CHAPTER TWENTY-EIGHT

THE NEXT DAY, LAUREN decided not to stop for her regular morning coffee visit with Elise and went straight to her office. Mid-morning, she looked up from the paperwork on the Thomas closing when her cell phone rang.

"I need to talk to you about something," Elise said before Lauren could even say hello. "Could you come over this evening? If you don't already have plans, that is."

Lauren put down her pen. "I'd love to. Even if I had plans, I'd break them if you needed me."

"Thank you. I'm sorry I've been preoccupied so much of the time lately. I've had a lot on my mind, busy with Andrea, work, and then that trip."

Lauren sighed. "I've missed you, that's for sure."

"I've missed you too." Lauren heard Elise pause and take a deep breath. "Anyway, we need to talk about some things, and I'd like to do it in person."

Lauren sat back in her chair as she bit her lower lip and took a breath of her own. "That sounds serious. Is everything okay?"

"Yes, I'm all right. I'm fine, actually." At least Elise didn't sound upset about anything.

Lauren sat back up. "Well, okay then. What time would you like me to be there?"

"Seven sounds good, if you can make it. If you can't, then just say when. And Lauren, I can never repay you for all I've been putting you through lately."

"I'll be there at seven. And, by the way, you haven't put me through anything I didn't want to do."

"I know, but...anyway I'll talk to you tonight."

"Right. See you at seven."

"Okay. Bye."

What in the world does Elise want to talk to me about? She sounded serious when she said, 'we need to talk.' Even though Elise said she was okay, when someone says, 'we need to talk' it's not usually a good thing. That's what Sharon told me when she was breaking up with me and moving back to Denver. That's what Carole said when she told me she had stage four cancer and was going to die soon.

Lauren tried to simply let it go and stop imagining the worst, but she couldn't help it. She holed up in her office. It got harder and harder to concentrate, so a few hours later she finally handed the paperwork over to her office manager to finish reviewing and left for home.

A while later, with the warm shower massage beating down on her shoulders and back, she leaned against the shower wall and tried to clear her mind of 'what if's' but they kept coming—each one worse than the previous. *She's going back to New York and not staying here. She said she was fine. What if that's just for my benefit? What if she isn't fine. Maybe she's decided she doesn't want a relationship with me, after all. Or with anyone. Or maybe she just wants to be friends and no more sleep-overs, even those innocent ones like we've had, and she wants me to take my stuff home. Please, God, don't let her be sick.*

She took another deep breath and tried again to clear her brain. It didn't work. She put her hands over her eyes and rubbed her face. *I love her. I love her. Oh, my God, I love her.* She leaned back against the shower tiles again and tried to will her heart to stop racing.

It's not that she couldn't live without her. It's not that her entire world would crumble if Elise told her it was over. It was, however, going to break her heart into a thousand tiny pieces if that happened, and it would take a long time to get over the pain. Lauren wished she'd been able to tell her how she felt about her, but she knew Elise would be scared off if she did. Telling her she loved her would not have been taking it as slow as Elise seemed to want it.

As she dried off after her shower, she examined her body. Things weren't right where she left them twenty years ago. Most had headed south or spread out. Lauren knew she was in good shape for her age. There was always that little bit added on for her age. Her waist was wider. Her stomach not quite as flat. The inside and outside of her thighs had some extra stuff that didn't live there some years ago. Her breasts weren't as perky as they once were and had already begun to sag a bit. Well, such is life. She found herself wishing she'd met Elise years ago after Carole died. *I was still marketable then. I don't feel very marketable now. Marketable...what a dumb thing to call yourself when you're only sixty-three.*

She still had several hours before she was due at Elise's. A nap would feel nice after the warm shower loosened her muscles. That round of tennis early this morning with one of her regular clients had been pushing it after last night's opening, but it had been fun.

She wrapped her robe around herself and sat on her bed. The plush white chenille bedspread was so soft, so inviting. She only needed to rest a bit, she thought. A catnap lying across her bed would be just the ticket. Remembering to set the alarm on her phone to wake her up, she grabbed a pillow from under the bedspread, pulled her legs up under her robe and curled herself into a near-fetal, comfortable position, trying to make her brain do likewise. As she drifted off, her brain kept running the same question in an endless loop: *Oh, Elise, what are you going to tell me?*

CHAPTER TWENTY-NINE

AT SEVEN ON THE dot, Lauren turned her Escalade into Elise's circular driveway. She found herself wondering if this was going to be the last time she did this. Her heart raced nearly as fast as her brain looking for a clue as to what Elise wanted to talk to her about. Before she could reach for Elise's front door handle Elise opened it and reached for her. Now her heart was racing for another reason. At least it didn't feel like a breakup embrace.

Instead, once they had stepped inside and closed the door, Elise pulled her close again and reached for a kiss. Their lips touched, and when Elise deepened the kiss, Lauren felt fire running through her entire body, heading south. Lauren squeezed her eyes closed tighter, swallowed hard, then opened them to find Elise's sapphire eyes regarding her.

"Wow, that was some kind of kiss."

Elise smiled and took Lauren's hand as she led her down the hall without a word spoken. That Lauren was confused was evident in her face. Elise stopped once and kissed her again, like she had by the door. Lauren's eyes got bigger, and she walked like she was in a trance.

Elise pushed open the bedroom doors, stopping at the foot of the bed, in front of the little white wicker settee. "It's time," was all she said. Elise unbuttoned one button on her blouse, then another. She reached for Lauren's hands, placing one on her breast as she said, "If you still want me, I want you."

Lauren's mouth fell open, she whispered, "I've wanted you for so long. Are you sure?"

Elise smiled. "I'm very sure."

***

Elise could feel Lauren's hands tremble a little as she slowly finished unbuttoning the rest of her blouse. She paused once, as if she was giving Elise one final chance to back out. Elise gave her another kiss

121

that left no doubt she wanted to continue. Lauren pushed the blouse off Elise's shoulders, letting it fall to the floor. Enclosed in Lauren's arms again, Elise closed her eyes as she felt Lauren's lips on hers, their tongues dancing together as the kiss deepened. Lauren trailed little kisses on the tender skin along Elise's jaw and down her neck to her shoulder.

Elise gasped at the feeling, tossing her head back, her mouth open. "Oh, God, that feels wonderful." Her heart was racing as Lauren unclasped her bra, pulling it to let it fall off her shoulders to the floor. Every touch stirred up what she had feared were long-dead embers, building up a fire that was beginning to burn once again after so many years. She hadn't been sure it was even there anymore, but there it was. It apparently merely needed to be stoked by the right partner. Stoked it was and it felt wonderful. She wanted more.

She took Lauren's face in her hands and kissed her deeply again. Each kiss seemed to reach deep inside her to her very center, leaving her almost breathless. When she came up for air, she reached for Lauren's polo shirt and pulled it over her head. Her hands stroked the skin of Lauren's sides and back as she marveled in the soft feel of her skin. *God, why did I wait so long for this?*

With every touch, she could hear Lauren's breathing quicken. She felt Lauren's hands on her own bare skin, exploring and reaching for the rest of her clothing. In minutes, she could feel something else she hadn't felt in years...she was becoming damp with desire.

Shortly, they were both naked as they made their way to the bed. Elise yanked the comforter down, tossing it onto the wicker settee at the foot. They both fell onto the bed, kissing and touching each other like two teenagers instead of the two sixty-somethings they actually were.

"You're so beautiful," Lauren whispered again and again as her hands lovingly caressed Elise's body.

Elise's throat constricted as her eyes filled with tears. This is what lovemaking should've always felt like. She couldn't remember the last time she felt this way, not even with...never mind. She gave herself over to simply feeling—purely touching and being touched.

Elise felt Lauren's kisses as she made her way down to her breasts, licking and caressing them one at a time. Her breathing was becoming ragged, her need more urgent. "Please," she begged, her voice husky with emotion.

As Lauren's mouth continued its southward exploration, her hand reached to caress Elise's behind. Her fingers trailed down the outside of her thighs, as her mouth reached that tender skin on the inside of her thighs.

"Oh, my God, Lauren. That feels so good." Elise moaned in pleasure at each touch and licked her lips, her eyes closed. Then she felt the pleasure of Lauren's fingers reaching for her center. She drew in a sharp breath as she felt her clit touched, then her own wetness as one of Lauren's fingers circled her entrance and dipped slightly in, then back up to her clit once more.

Lauren kissed her way back up to her ear, where she whispered, "I want you so much."

"Oh, yes. I want you too," she gasped out as she tried to breathe.

Elise felt Lauren reach a finger farther inside, and then back up to her clit again as her mouth returned to pleasuring Elise's breasts. She felt herself moving with each stroke, her breathing quickening as the feeling was building. Lauren's fingers were inside her, one, then two of them going after her pleasure spot, Lauren's thumb still caressing her clit, as the strokes quickened. A few moments later, Elise cried out her release, her back arching with Lauren's fingers still inside her. She could feel herself grabbing onto those fingers for dear life, pushing against Lauren's hand as another wave hit her.

Lauren's lips were on hers, softly, sweetly, as her arms encircled her. As she held her, Lauren whispered, "You've no idea how often I fantasized about this happening, hoping you'd want me like I want you. I was willing to wait as long as it took to experience this with you."

Elise knew for sure right then. No going back. She waited for her breathing to calm somewhat. Elise put her hand on Lauren's cheek and gazed directly into those beautiful grey eyes.

"Lauren, I love you. I've loved you for a while now but was afraid to tell you." She waited for a response, nervous and excited at the same time. She didn't have long to wait. The response was almost instantaneous.

"Oh, honey, I love you, too." Lauren placed a kiss on Elise's lips, pulling her closer for an embrace. "I knew I loved you. I didn't want to scare you off, either." She shook her head and looked back at her. "What a pair we are. To tell you the truth, every other time someone has said to me 'we have to talk,' it was leading to something bad. My head was full of what-ifs on the way over here and I was afraid of what I would walk into when I got here." She stroked Elise's hair, kissed her forehead, and looked back into her eyes. "I was worried you were going to tell me to pack my things and take a hike. In a nice way of course. I was afraid you were going to break my heart. I love you so much, sweetheart."

"All I can say now is that I wish I hadn't been so afraid of this kind of intimacy. I was afraid you wouldn't want me as I am now. I'm not young anymore."

"But you're wonderful as you are now. Neither of us is as we were in our twenties or even forties, you know. You're everything I want. You're sweet and sexy and smart and I knew I was falling for you the first time I saw you. Pretty bad, huh?"

"Not at all. I think it's very sweet. I do have another confession to make. That two weeks I was gone, um...I was at a spa in New York. Body wraps, the whole thing. I knew I wanted you, and I wanted to give you the best version of me that I could."

"You didn't need to do that. I've seen you in a bathing suit, so I knew what most of you looked like." Lauren softly stroked Elise's cheek. "Believe me, you're beautiful as you are. If you wanted to do that for yourself, then fine. But, honey, you never have to do that for me."

"Thank you. I do appreciate that, but it did make me feel better and gave me a bit more courage. There was one other thing on my end. I was also afraid I couldn't..." She smiled faintly. "I guess that's definitely been blown out of the water."

"Uh, yeah...definitely." Lauren laughed her throaty Lauren Bacall laugh as her hand made its way back to the damp place it had recently been.

"Mmm...well, if you think this is over, it isn't." Elise reached for Lauren, her next kiss giving Lauren a hint of what was in store for her.

CHAPTER THIRTY

FOUR MONTHS LATER

THREE COUPLES. ONE POOL party at Elise's house. One little dog dozing by the pool, having had her fill of grilled hot dogs.

"All right, Elise. You've survived your first summer in Florida, hurricane season and all the changing seasons, such as they are here. Still happy with your decision to make this your year-round home and give up your status as a Snowbird?" Shawn asked.

Elise smiled at her from her position on the pool float, trailing one hand in the water. "Definitely. Besides, now that Andrea isn't running a gallery in New York any more, she wouldn't have as much of a reason to visit except to visit me. Now that we both live here, it's nice to be able to see all of you whenever we want to."

"Well, I'm happy about it, for sure," Lauren chimed in. "Now that I've seen Elise's home in New York I can see why she was reluctant to leave." She looked at Elise. "I'm glad you're keeping it. It's gorgeous and still homey. It also has a lot of great memories, not to mention that astounding view."

Andi sat up on her lounge chair. "I love your New York home. I admit I was dreading the day you decided to let it go. Most of my childhood was spent there. At least for now, we can spend time there when we want to. I'm sure someday you'll be ready to sell it to some other family but for now, I'm grateful you're keeping it."

"Speaking of keeping things, how are you feeling about giving up SoHo?" Carrie asked. "You've had a little while to get used to the idea."

Andi sat back in the lounger. "Making the final decision was the hard part. A compromise was the best idea. Lauren's idea of selling two-thirds of the SoHo gallery to Michael and David was a more comfortable move for me at the time. I couldn't make myself give it up entirely, at least not yet. We have written into the agreement that when I'm ready, they'll buy me out completely. For now, becoming a silent partner still gives me the feeling of being part of it without having to make any decisions on a day-to-day basis. All I have to run right now is Heartwood, and that's plenty. Lauren's other idea that I should just handle the artists, the part I love most, and hire a store manager for the rest is working out perfectly for me."

"It does seem to agree with you," Carrie said. "It's been an interesting summer, that's for sure. We're so glad you're back to doing whatever you want. I doubt I could keep up with you nowadays, and I didn't have a heart attack."

"That cardio rehab did me a world of good." Andi reached for the pina colada on the table next to her. "I've been making the effort to stay active and I've started running again. I feel like I'm completely past what happened, then again, I won't take my good health for granted anymore."

Andi and Kelly exchanged a look between them. When Andi smiled and nodded at her, Kelly said, "Andi and I would like to make an announcement." She reached for Andi's hand and kissed the back of it before she continued. "I was sure, before Andi came along, that I wasn't destined to find the love that Shawn writes about in her romance novels—the kind of love that Shawn and Carrie found. I never thought this could happen to me. But it did." She looked over at Andi and smiled. "Last night I asked this beautiful, wonderful woman to marry me, and she said yes. All that's left is for Elise to give us her blessing."

There was a round of wows and congratulations, rousing Piper to leap up and down and bark. Shawn jumped up and hugged her best friend, and then she hugged Andi as well. "I'm very happy for both of you."

Carrie picked up Piper and hugged them both, then to Kelly she said, "I told Andi you were a knight in shining armor, and now you're hers. I couldn't be happier for both of you."

"I think we know who'll be babysitting Piper when we take our honeymoon," Kelly said, looking pointedly at her dog. "Whose dog are you anyway?" She laughed as she retrieved Piper and began scratching her ears.

Elise and Lauren had pulled themselves out of the pool and wrapped themselves in beach towels. Elise made her way to Andi and Kelly and gave each of them a kiss on the cheek. "I'd hug you, but I don't want to get you wet. I'm very happy for both of you. Andrea, it couldn't have pleased me more than for you to find true happiness for yourself. Kelly, you became a good friend right away, and I'm more than delighted to welcome you officially into the family, as if you weren't already anyway. I know you two are meant to be together and heartily give you my blessing."

Lauren clapped Kelly on the shoulder. "We've been friends for a long time now, and I've always hoped you'd find real love and settle down. Looks like you have, and I'm thrilled for you both." She put her arm around Elise. "It's wonderful to see two young couples in love, isn't it?"

Shawn put her arm around Carrie. "Three couples in love. None of us are kids anymore. Still, there's nothing like a real life 'happily ever after,' is there?"

THE END

SPONTANEOUS CORONARY ARTERY DISSECTION (SCAD)

The condition I referred to in this book, Spontaneous Coronary Artery Dissection, or SCAD, is real. It's rare, although some researchers have suggested that it might be more common than reported. It can occur in men or women, but it happens mostly to younger women usually within an age range of thirty to fifty, with an average age of forty-two. A number of the women studied had recently given birth.

Researchers have been looking for a genetic mutation that might cause this. However, they haven't located one as of this writing. They recently identified a possible genetic connection to some connective tissue disorders. So far that hasn't been absolutely verified, either. There are very few instances of familial connections, but they have occurred and can't be ruled out.

The symptoms of SCAD include: Chest pain, rapid or fluttery heartbeat feeling in your chest, pain in your arms, jaw, or shoulder, shortness of breath, nausea, dizziness, and unusual, extreme tiredness.

If you experience any of the above symptoms and suspect a heart attack, please don't wait. Call emergency services (911 in the USA) and seek medical attention immediately. Only drive yourself to the emergency room as an absolute last resort.

If you'd like to research this disease further, you can begin with these:

www.scadresearch.org/about

http://www.mayoclinic.org/diseases-conditions/spontaneous-coronary-artery-dissection/symptoms-causes/syc-20353711

http://www.heart.org/HEARTORG/Conditions/HeartAttack/AboutHeart Attacks/Spontaneous-Coronary-Artery-Dissection-Not-Just-a-Heart-Attack_UCM_454434_Article.jsp

About BJ Phillips

I've been writing practically since I've been reading. People who knew me well knew my biggest dream and biggest fear was writing a whole book. That fear of failure. I had poetry published in my school literary magazine and a funny story in my work professional magazine. I wrote training materials for work and helped friends write their resumes, feeling that was at least writing. I had the beginnings of fantasy stories, mysteries, and love stories all sitting in folders and notebooks.

In the summer of 2013 I saw the National Novel Writing Month (NaNoWriMo) challenge. If you're not familiar with it, the challenge is to write 50,000 words in 30 days. The day after Thanksgiving that year, I posted 51,000 words and a complete story was born. It needed a lot of work, but it was there. That story was the bones of Hurricane Season, my debut novel, which was published June 2016.

Early in 2014, I heard about a new program through the Golden Crown Literary Society (GCLS) called the Writing Academy. It's a one-year program aimed at new writers or writers who want to improve their skills. I'm proud to be part of the very first graduating class.

The Writing Academy was life-changing. I started looking at myself as an author, not just as someone who happens to write. I retired the beginning of 2015. I became a full-time writer of stories and finally finished my first book the end of July 2015.

I live in Florida with my partner, a retired police officer, Maya the Yorkie, and Piper the Chihuahua in an honest-to-goodness resort—it says so on the sign out front. When I'm not writing, we love sitting out on the front porch with the "kids" and chatting with neighbors and friends who like to come by and visit. I'm an avid reader of anything that strikes my fancy and I love puzzles – like logic problems, Sudoku or word finds. I also like to take walks, go to flea markets, sketch, and crochet. Okay, I'm also addicted to several TV shows, mostly mysteries and cop shows. Thank goodness for the DVR!

I'm very excited about becoming part of the Desert Palm Press family. I have several books in the pipeline right now, a murder mystery and another romance.

Connect with BJ

Email: bjphillipswrites@gmail.com

Website: www.bjphillipsauthor.com

Twitter: https//twitter.com/bjwrites01

Other Books by BJ Phillips

Hurricane Season

ISBN: 9781942976134

Shawn Richards (aka S.K. Richardson) is a romance author. She's had her heart broken badly again and is done with love. Ditching San Francisco, she moves back home to Southwest Florida to get her feet back under her and finish her latest novel.

Carrie Alexander is a huge S.K. Richardson fan, but has no idea what she looks like. She does, however, like the looks of the new neighbor down the street, Shawn Richards.

Drawn to each other as friends, Shawn still tries to keep some distance despite what she's beginning to feel for Carrie. Carrie isn't the kind of woman you just have a fun night with and then move on. Carrie's the kind you fall in love with and make love to, and live happily ever after with—but she just can't let herself trust her heart yet. After all, the last time she fell for one of her fans, it ended badly.

Carrie is looking for 'happy ever after' just like in all those romance novels she reads. Shawn could be the one, or maybe Carrie's fooling herself and there's really no such thing as all that romantic stuff in Shawn's books.

Shawn is afraid she can't deliver on that 'happy ever after' she knows Carrie wants—and she wants, too, truth be told. Destiny might have given them a push when Carrie tripped at the local grocery store and literally fell into Shawn's arms. But fear could cost Shawn the woman of her dreams.

Snowbird Season

ISBN: 9781942976448

In this sequel to *Hurricane Season*, Kelly Bradley is nearly forty and feels destined to always be alone. She meets Andi Wainwright, niece of Snowbird Elise Wainwright, while doing a woodworking job. There is an attraction, but Andi is healing from a failed relationship.

How can Andi, a woman from New York City and owner of an art gallery in SoHo, and Kelly, a middle-class Florida Girl who has no intention of ever living anywhere else, make it work?

Note to Readers:

Thank you for reading a book from Desert Palm Press. We have made every effort to edit this book. However, typos do slip in. If you find an error in the text, please email lee@desertpalmpress.com so the issue can be corrected.

We appreciate you as a reader and want to ensure you enjoy the reading process. We would like you to consider posting a review on your preferred media sites such as Amazon, Smashwords, Bella Books, Goodreads, Tumblr, Twitter, Facebook, and/or your blog or website.

For more information on upcoming releases, author interviews, contest, giveaways and more, please sign up for our newsletter and visit us as at Desert Palm Press: www.desertpalmpress.com and "Like" us on Facebook: Desert Palm Press.

Bright Blessings

www.ingramcontent.com/pod-product-compliance
Lightning Source LLC
Chambersburg PA
CBHW070824250626
47170CB00006B/2207